# WISHING FOR A DUKE

*A Time-Travel Regency Romance*

Susanne Marie Knight

**Romance Writing with a Twist**

http://romancewritingwithatwist.blogspot.com

http:/www.susanneknight.com

# Dedication

To Shelley,

Who showed me the way back!

# Reviewer Praise For
# Susanne Marie Knight and
# WISHING FOR A DUKE

\* *Dream Realm Award-Winner for Best Speculative Fiction Romance;*

\* *Preditor and Editor Award Winner for Best Science Fiction Novel;*

\* *Awe-Struck Award Winner for Best Novel;*

\* *Golden Wings Award Winner for Best Historical Romance;*

\* *Seven times finalist in the prestigious EPIC eBook Awards;*

\* *Amazon Best-selling author.*

\* Susanne Marie Knight is a talented, versatile author whose books run from light traditional Regency with a magical element, to time-travel, sci-fi romance, paranormal romantic suspense, mystery, and contemporary romance. Jane Bowers, *Romance Reviews Today.*

\* Absolutely splendid! Mature, balanced, and imaginative; a balanced prose style. J. Manchester*, New York critic.*

\* 5 Stars! Every page delights! WISHING FOR A DUKE had us wishing for more. Ms. Knight explores the inequity between the haves--aristocracy, and the have-nots--the servants. In this time-travel Regency, a modern woman gets a little help from her friends to heal from a past trauma. The Duke's son, Robbie, is pure gold and a surprise connection links the past and the present! A very fun read!-- *Regency Fiction World*

\* 5 Kisses! Pure heaven. Here is another Susanne Marie Knight time-travel Regency to binge on! Make a wish on a daisy, throw in a little Thyme, a hypnotic beat here, a village healer there, and voilà! You have all the fixings for a high-in-the-instep Duke to fall in love with a twenty-first century beautician. Will he ask her to become his Duchess? Will she say yes? Find out for yourself in WISHING FOR A DUKE.!- *-The Romance Guide*

# Prologue

## Current Year

From Elaina Wattell's vantage point, lying on the grass in the park adjacent to her mother's apartment building, she gazed up at the cerulean skies of a warm August day. Fleecy clouds dotted the brilliant blue above her. Things were as perfect as could be. And why not? Everything that she'd been working for these past two years was almost in her grasp.

Almost. She was so excited she could hardly keep still on the picnic blanket. But she didn't want to jinx herself or her good fortune. She didn't have to be nervous. Her new hair salon was almost in the bag.

As if to dispute her thoughts, a crow, magnificent with its uniform black feathers, disturbed the quiet with a loud, droning caw. Several caws. It fluttered its wings, and then lifted up from the overhead oak tree's branches. She watched it majestically fly out into the sun.

"Don't you wish that you could soar like a bird?" Leila Johnson, lying next to Elaina, swept her arm up and out to encompass the dazzling hue of a tranquil blue sky. "Rise up and fly over the rainbow to escape the madness? Soar up there and be free?"

Elaina looked over at her friend and shook her head. "No, I don't. First of all, it's a clear day; there is no rainbow, right? And tell me, why would I want to escape when I'm on the verge of getting exactly what I want? Exactly what I've been working for?"

"Oh, you." Leila lifted up onto an elbow and swatted at Elaina's shoulder. "Rub it in. It's your birthday, you're moving into the loft above the new hair salon you've been planning on launching for ages, and, not to forget, you're going to get a proposal from a Duke."

Elaina rocketed up from her reclined position. She had to set her friend straight. "It's not that kind of proposal, Leila. Jimmy and Nathan Duke, cousins you know, are talking about financing my startup costs, helping me get the permits I need. Things like that. There's nothing romantic about it. Besides, they're rather ruthless; they certainly don't mix business with pleasure. But..."

She couldn't help sighing. "Yep, I *am* wishing on a Duke. For a Duke. Wishing one of the cousins... or both... come through with their promise to get my salon business up and operating."

Going from a stylist in a stable of stylists to a sole ownership was a big deal. A huge deal. But Leila knew that; they'd known each forever. Ever since Elaina's second birthday, with Leila ringing in two years older.

Now, today, Elaina turned twenty-four. And yep, things were going her way for sure. She'd secured an excellent location for her business on the Lower East Side; her building stood in the shadow of the stately Manhattan Bridge. Maybe not the lowest crime area, but the rent was affordable, in addition to having the loft upstairs. Nearby were the neighborhoods of Chinatown, Little Italy, and, not too far away, Greenwich Village, so there were plenty of trendy, upscale customers to frequent her full-service salon.

All she had to do was get the word out. "Get Pampered" was her new shop's name. Or it would be the name once all the licenses and permits were in place.

The only thing she didn't like about it was that she'd be living by herself, at least for a while. After college, she'd moved from her mom's apartment to a two-bedroom walk-up with three roommates. Crowded, but fun. Now though, when she moved again, it would be only her in the loft. Honestly, there wasn't enough room for anyone else.

She shivered. Being on her own would be... a challenge, especially because she was still in therapy after... after what had happened when she was just a toddler, but she'd manage. She'd gotten her therapy sessions down to once every other month. She'd conquer her fears; she'd be just fine.

Leila also sat up. She brushed bits of grass and dirt from her gorgeous mane of highlighted, or, to use a stylist's word, balayage colored hair. One of Elaina's specialties was balayage treatments for long hair, and Leila had been a guinea pig--a happy guinea pig, thankfully. Her long tresses had been transformed from an ebony brown color graduating to a pale champagne blonde down to the ends. With her long gold hoop earrings, she looked *très* exotic.

Beautiful!

Elaina's own hair remained virgin chestnut brown, but maybe one of these days, she'd give herself a balayage, too.

Leila tugged on Elaina's arm. "Wait. It's quiet here in the park. I have a perfect idea for what we can do before Tessa, your mom, tells us she's ready for us to come up to her apartment. We have two hours before the celebration begins, right?"

Then, oddly enough, Leila spaced out, staring at a few children having fun in the nearby playground. She seemed to be lost in thought as she watched the group of kids with their happy antics.

Elaina could understand the distraction. Swings, monkey bars, slides, sandbox, running through the sprinklers on this hot August day... these were wonderful reminders of the joys of childhood.

Leila then came back to life. "Listen, I've gotta say I think it's really odd that Tessa wants to recreate the party she gave you when you were two... except that it'll be in her apartment, instead of being on a campout. Actually, that's a kinda creepy idea."

"Yep, it's pretty strange, for sure. But Mom's insisting on doing it this way. She's invited everyone who'd been there at the campgrounds twenty-two years ago. You, neighbor twins Johnny and Patty--they must be twenty-nine now, and also my cousin, Carrie, who's thirty-one." Elaina shrugged. "Mom still feels guilty about the... you know, the accident."

"Yeah, I was only four so I don't really remember it, but my mom always talks about how you were found in a ravine three days later."

*Awake but in deep shock.* Honestly, Elaina hadn't opened her mouth to speak for almost a year afterwards--at least that was what her mom always said. But that was so very long ago. Elaina took a deep breath to keep that trauma buried.

"Anyway, this is what I had in mind, *mi chica.*" Leila toyed with a crystal pendant around her neck. "I've been studying self-hypnosis... on my own, y'know. You remember I told you one of my long ago ancestors used to dabble in the stuff. Anyway, I had an idea that I might be able to help you... plus, you could be *my* guinea pig. How about if I hypnotize you?"

Hypnosis? Elaina felt as if her stomach dropped. The very idea of that gave her a major case of *agita*.

"It's quiet here, *chica,* and peaceful. No one can really see us under this copse of trees or hear us speak. I'll just go into the script, and you try to relax and follow along. Maybe, just maybe I can fix you." Leila fluffed out her flowing hair. "Wouldn't that be a super birthday present?"

"Well--"

"C'mon, you. Let me do it. It's meant to be. Just look at this."

She reached around the trunk of the huge oak tree and pulled out a leafy, green... and fragrant shrub. The aroma in the air was like something from a French chef's kitchen: pleasant, pungent, earthy.

"It's the herb thyme, Elaina! My grand-grams all down the line used this herb a lot. It's sort of like a family tradition. Anyway, thyme is supposed to help with courage and raise our vibrations to a higher level. It's also supposed to protect against psychic vampires."

"Psychic vampires! Well, we don't want any of those, do we?" Elaina bowed to the inevitable; she knew her friend wouldn't give up so she got comfortable on the squishy grass under the blanket. Heaving a deep breath, she then folded her hands across her tummy.

Her blue jeans, frayed on the edges, and her sleeveless, scooped-neck top allowed the summer breezes to travel up her bare arms, to tickle her ankles and toes, and to twirl a strand or two of her loose hair about her face.

"Okay. I'm ready. Do your worst. Or rather, you'd better do your best, Leila!"

"Wait, wait. I found something else." Leila reached around the trunk of the tree in the other direction and pulled something else out of the ground.

She handed over a green-stemmed white daisy. "It's a wishing daisy. Y'know, 'He loves me, he loves me not.' You pluck the petals and make a wish. I'll get myself in the zone, and then we'll begin."

"Sure." Elaina rolled her eyes but took the daisy.

What would she wish for other than the Dukes' supporting her business? Shrugging, she concentrated on the "He loves me, he loves me not" portion of the daisy tradition.

As her friend gave instructions about being comfortable and relaxed, about being peaceful and open to healing, Elaina finished with the daisy petals. She ended up on the glorious phrase: "He loves me."

Good. At least that was out of the way.

Lying there on the blanket, she allowed herself to drift on her friend's soft and monotone voice.

Some kind of vibration sounds floated through the air; Leila had selected this "music" from her phone. "This'll relax you, okay? It's a mix of delta wave frequencies and it helps with healing and deep-seated pain. It also accesses your unconscious mind."

"Cool," Elaina murmured. Honestly, she thought all this was a bunch of mumbo-jumbo.

But...

Hmmn. She did feel peaceful so she adjusted her sunglasses resting on her nose and concentrated on breathing.

The sounds of chirping birds, the thunder of a passing Metro-North commuter train, and the laughter from children in the playground all faded in the distance. Even the aroma of thyme seemed to grow fainter.

"Close your eyes, Elaina, and take three slow, deep breaths. Focus on what you want. What you need to heal yourself. Focus on your wish."

A strange thought invaded Elaina's wellbeing: *wishing for a Duke*. Maybe that was what she'd use the wishing daisy for. She couldn't help smiling. That was what she'd said to Leila just a few minutes ago.

"Now I'm gonna count from ten to zero, Elaina. And when I finish, you'll be back in the past where you need to be healed. I'll ask you some questions, and you'll answer me. And then, when we're done, I'll count up to three, and you'll come out of the trance. Okay? Do you hear me?"

"Yes. Yes, I hear you." Elaina continued to take long breaths as she listened to her friend's countdown from ten to zero.

Once zero was reached, Leila must've leaned in closer because Elaina felt warm breath dance across her face. "Elaina, tell me. What do you see?"

Elaina felt her eyelids flutter. "I see... children. Young children. Johnny and Carrie. Patty and you. I see me. I have tears in my eyes. I see... I see..."

Nothing. The picture from the past disappeared and she saw nothing. Felt nothing. Tasted nothing. Heard nothing, not even the delta wave frequency. It was as if she was in a void.

The only sense that was alive was the sense of smell. She smelled the aroma of thyme.

And then, there was nothing again. She completely passed out.

# Chapter One

## Where Was She?

Elaina woke up to an insistent tugging on the lower edge of her sleeveless top.

"What the...?" She opened her eyes to see the startling blue-eyed gaze of a young boy with a mop of curly nutmeg brown hair staring at her.

"Good-O!" he crowed. "You're awake! I shall keep you! What an excellent stroke of good luck!"

He released her top and then stood over her with his small fists placed against his tiny hips. "Ho!" he called out into the forest surrounding them, obviously not afraid to raise his voice.

Then he lifted his head up toward the overhead azure blue sky and shouted, "Wait 'til Edgars sees what I found on the grounds!" He then looked down at her. "Edgars is the head gardener. He's always telling me there are no surprises in the gardens, not since he's tended Wolfeshire Park, but ha! I sure found one! You!"

Elaina shook her head to try and clear it. Where in the world was she? While Leila, with a monotone voice, had read her script, Elaina must've fallen into some kind of trance, some kind of sleep.

She wrinkled her nose. No, that couldn't have been right. After all they'd both been together in the city park right by her mother's apartment. She looked around. Leila... well, she certainly wasn't here now.

But, where in the world was here? The nearby flanking trees weren't of the familiar oak variety like the ones she'd sat under to take shelter from the afternoon sun. These trees, majestic and huge-trunked, were gnarled together, huddled closely as if afraid to strike out on their own.

Were they beech trees? European beech trees? No matter, whatever they were, their branches with verdant green leaves reached over to touch their fellow trees as if protecting themselves from being alone.

Elaina could relate to that whimsical thought.

Truthfully though, her surroundings were primitive, elemental, overwhelming... almost spooky. In no way, shape, or form were these trees like those memorable oaks in her neighborhood park.

And oh, by the way, where was Leila?

Elaina glanced up at the boy. Before she had a chance to ask him a question, a frown turned down his rosebud lips.

He looked at her with a quizzical expression and hopped all around her as she sat. "Tell me, girl, why are you here at the Park, dressed in your undergarments?"

Sitting up, Elaina wrapped her arms around her bent knees and looked up at this active little boy. She was decently dressed--jeans and a top; in all her years she'd never had her summer clothes mistaken for underwear.

This boy... not only did he have a British accent, but he was dressed so oddly, like an anachronism: with a loose, long sleeved white shirt, and baggy knee-length breeches with a flap in the front, not a zipper. His shirttails were untucked from his pants to then freely flutter in the breeze.

Sticking out of his unruly hair were twigs and leaves, almost as many as if he'd planted them in his mass of curls himself. As if he were a hybrid between a Human boy and a piece of shrubbery! He looked quite wild, untamed.

She doubted that he had decorated his hair that way. His angelic face protested his innocence.

No. Not angelic. She wouldn't be fooled by his innocent looks. This lean boy, perhaps six or seven, was probably a mischievous devil in disguise.

The devil spoke. "I asked you a question, girl. It's your duty to answer me." He lifted his chin as if he was used to adults obeying his childish commands.

She smiled. "You're right. Sorry. But first I think we should introduce ourselves. I'm Elaina Wattell." She held her hand up for a shake.

The boy stared at her hand for a moment, and then shook it forcefully. "I'm... Robert Burnley." He then grinned. "Yes, you may call me Robert."

How regal! She grinned back at him. "How about if I call you Robbie?"

His eyebrows met at the bridge of his well-formed nose. "Robbie? No one's ever..." He darted his bright-eyed gaze to the left, then right, and then nodded. "Yes. Good. You may call me Robbie."

What a pip! "So, Robbie, where is this place? I was with my friend and then all of a sudden, boom, I woke up here."

She had no clue about what had happened. After all, it wasn't typical to fall asleep in the company of a best friend and then wake up in an entirely different place. Even the air smelled different, better: fresher, purer, full of natural scents.

Wait. What time was it? What about her birthday party? Was she late? Had her mother called to remind her and Leila?

Without thinking, Elaina glanced around at where she sat. No blanket and no cute, colorful handbag in sight, and that meant... her smart phone, wallet, apartment keys were... She swallowed a ragged breath... were stolen.

*Oh no. Oh good gosh.*

Fear plummeted down into her lowest levels. What had happened? Did she somehow walk or stumble into the forested area of the park? Or had she been abducted? Hit on the head and pirated away?

Was it a long ways back to her mother's apartment?

Never mind that. *Where was Leila?*

Robbie touched Elaina's bare upper arm. "Your garments, girl. Why are you not wearing a proper morning gown? Were your clothes stolen? And your feet! Why, your toes are showing. I've never seen footwear like that." He shook his head, scattering his tree-infested hair. "And your spectacles, I've never seen black lenses. Are you blind?"

"Don't call me 'girl'. My name's Elaina." Sure, she was a little curt with him, but honestly, didn't she have a reason to be?

Oh what a monumental headache.

Standing, she smoothed down the material on her shirt, brushed back her loose hair, and then set her sunglasses on top of her head. "These are sunglasses, okay? I'm not blind. And where I'm from, jeans and a top are what's usually worn in hot weather."

She wiggled her toes. "These are sandals. I mean, it's summer, isn't it?"

"Summer, yes. August. I shall call you Elle." He then shrugged his puny shoulders. "This is my home. Wolfeshire Park. The Duke lives here. It's one of his many estates."

Duke? Which one, Jimmy or Nathan? Did they somehow bundle her up in a car and then leave her out in the wilderness? But why would they want to do that?

This whole thing was so very odd... and scary... and well, honestly, it was a mystery, and that certainly wasn't what she wanted for her birthday.

But at least she wasn't alone.

Robbie grabbed at his midsection. "Oh, I'm as hungry as a hunter! Let's go back to the Main Hall. Perhaps it's time for supper. I hope so. I'm done with running away... for right now, anyway."

Her stomach growled as if answering him.

He held out his hand and wiggled his fingers. "Come... Elle. You're with me. I'll make sure you get fed."

"Thanks." She wrinkled her nose. What a strange little boy. Rather full of himself, wasn't he?

Taking his small hand, Elaina increased her pace to keep up with him. He pulled her along as if she were a recalcitrant dog on a leash. Wherever they were headed, she was sure she'd get some answers to her immensely important questions. And then, one way or another, she'd hitch a ride back to her mother's apartment.

**✱ ✱ ✱ ✱**

If Elaina thought she'd get her questions answered, she was sadly, sadly mistaken. In addition to whatever questions she had before, she now had a gazillion more. Oh yeah, her mind was reeling.

Robbie had led her to a back entrance of a huge house. A mansion, really. Or a mansion's mansion. Honestly, she'd never seen anything as big or as grand.

After opening the solid wooden door, he pulled her through into a lobby or entryway of some sort. The inside wasn't as impressive as the outside. Once the door had closed, the quiet of nature's physical rhythm was at an end, now replaced with a jumble of household noises.

Someone, an older woman with frizzy grey curls, a frumpy hat, and a roomy gown jumped up from a chair set against the unadorned plaster walls. "Master Robert! Where 'ave ye been? I've been lookin' everywhere for ye!"

The woman's shaky voice could scarcely be heard above the hubbub around them. As if there was a Christmas sale going on, men and women dressed in old-fashioned clothes rushed past them, to and fro, and back again. The women wore long dresses in the sprightly colors of black and grey, along with white aprons, and the men had dingy stockings and baggy breeches with very long vests. These folks scurried about the corridor, obviously busy, but not too busy to stare at Elaina, or rather, they stared at what she was wearing.

Honestly, she felt almost naked, even though she was completely covered except for her arms. What was wrong with these people? Oddly enough, none of them paid any attention to the little boy by her side.

"Master Robert!" The grey-haired woman squeezed the boy to her matronly breasts in an obviously unwanted hug. "Ye be the death o'me. Yer ol'nanny has been in queer stirrups since ye been a-hidin' from me."

Robbie wiggled his way out of the woman's grasp. "Don't be silly, Price. I told you, it's tedious in the house with no one to amuse me. So outside, I played hide and go seek... by myself, and look what I found?"

He held up Elaina's hand as if she was a trophy.

Elaina pulled her arm away. "Listen, um, ma'am, I'm a bit confused. I woke up--"

"Ack! Oh, my eyes!" The woman's watery eyes widened and she squawked, "Wot ever will we do? This... This doxy be soilin' Wolfeshire Park."

Doxy? What? Elaina straightened her back. "Hey now. Wait just one minute--"

"Madam," a deep, sonorous male voice carried down the corridor.

Elaina turned toward the voice. Walking towards them was a rather grand personage wearing dark trousers, a dark tailcoat, a shiny satin vest, white gloves, and a fancy bunch of cloth around his neck. His salt and pepper hair slicked back, his grizzled sideburns long and fuzzy, he had a look of distaste on his ruddy face.

The man stopped in front of Elaina, gazed down his large nose at her, and then snapped his fingers.

Someone suddenly appeared by the man's side. A younger man in similar clothing who might've been the same age as Elaina, handed the first man a woolen blanket. The older man then draped it around her shoulders.

"Now, Madam, follow me. I will have a word with you in the pantry."

Yikes. She felt like she was going to get scolded. But this man probably had the answers she was looking for. Holding the blanket close against her chest, she turned to go along with him.

Robbie pulled on one of the man's black tails. "Mr. Doyle, wait. This is Elle. She's mine. I found her. She's a good egg, and hungry, too. As am I. Mrs. Parsons is making something special for me, I can just smell it. I want to share my supper with Elle."

The man, Mr. Doyle, sniffed. "Young sir, you shall go forthwith to your bedchamber. Directly. No stops. A bath is being prepared for you. After you are clean, and only after that, you may enjoy the supper Cook has prepared for you... alone."

Robbie stomped his foot. "No! You're only the butler. I don't have to listen to you. My father--"

"Your father has left me the honor of dealing with you when you... shall we say, misbehave?" Mr. Doyle leveled a stern gaze. "Now, Master Robert, accompany your nanny up to your bedchamber."

The boy made such a comical pouting face, complete with protruding lips and rolling eyes. Elaina wanted to laugh, only Robbie really did need a firm hand. Laughing would be rewarding his bad behavior... or rather, misbehavior, to use Mr. Doyle's words.

She gave a wave of goodbye to Robbie and then headed out of the entryway with Mr. Doyle for parts unknown. She actually had learned something during the battle of words between Robbie and Mr. Doyle. This humungous residence employed a nanny, a cook, a head gardener, and a butler, among plenty of other staff members.

**\* \* \* \***

The butler led the way down a long corridor and past many open doors. One doorway revealed a frenetic kitchen. It also emitted scrumptious aromas.

In response, Elaina's tummy growled.

Mr. Doyle then turned right into a suite of rooms, the first of which was a beautifully organized area filled with wine racks, crystal goblets, fine china, and a wall safe. This must've been the pantry. Truthfully, it was a very impressive room. With all the wood cabinets and paneling on the walls, it also absorbed whatever sounds were made by the commotion outside.

Like Robbie's howling. As he made his way to his room, his wail of displeasure followed him. Honestly, the child's crying was almost eardrum-splitting in intensity.

Mr. Doyle sat behind a polished wooden desk and indicated for her to stand in front of him. Evidently, he wasn't going to offer her a chair.

She shrugged. Ah well. Pulling the blanket tighter around her, she broke the silence. "Listen, Mr. Doyle, there's been a misunderstanding--"

"Madam." His small eyes narrowed as he looked at her. "State what your business is at Wolfeshire Park."

She nibbled on her lower lip. "That's just it. I don't have business here. I was someplace else, resting on the grass in a city park. I-I fell asleep, and then when I woke up, I was here, in these woods. Robbie found me."

"Master Robert," the man corrected.

She skewed her lips. "Sure. So, where is this place? How far am I from the city?"

The man cleared his throat. "The city lies to the north of Wolfeshire Park, as the crow flies. Fifty miles."

"What?" Fifty miles north was New York City?

She took a deep breath and visualized a map of the tri-state area. Did this mean she was in New Jersey? Maybe around the oceanside resort of Asbury Park? But how could that be? How in the world...

The sting of tears burned her eyes so she rapidly blinked them. How did this happen to her?

"Madam." Mr. Doyle stood and then moved a small bench over for her to sit on. "You have had a shock. May I pour you a glass of sherry?"

"No, no, but thank you." She sat, slumped her shoulders, and massaged her forehead.

What was she going to do? The only thing she could think of was to use the phone here and call her mother, or Leila, and have them or someone come pick her up.

Yep, this was an emergency times ten.

She heaved a heavy breath. But still, it wasn't so bad. She could get her identification replaced. Cancel her smart phone and credit cards. Replace her keys. Things like that. It wouldn't be such a big deal.

"Madam," the butler said again as he returned to his seat behind the desk. "What is your profession?"

Honestly, what did that have to do with anything? "I'm a hairstylist. You know, snip, snip." She imitated scissors with her fingers. "Soon, very soon, I'm opening my own full-service salon."

Fingers crossed. This "little" detour was bound to set her back, but for just how long, it was hard to tell.

Mr. Doyle solemnly nodded. "I see. A coiffeur, or rather a coiffeuse. Are you French?"

That was a non-sequitur! "No, American. Why?"

He sat back in his chair and linked his stubby fingers together, resting his hands over his chest. "For some inexplicable reason, the Bon Ton favor the French style over the English. If you do intend to open shop, I advise you to be addressed as a *mademoiselle*. *Mademoiselle* Elle, is that correct?"

"Oh, I forgot to introduce myself. I'm Elaina Wattell." She extended her arm across the desk to shake his hand.

He looked surprised but completed the handshake. "*Mademoiselle* Elaina, yes?" In a low voice he muttered something about the title adding respectability.

With that out of the way, she got to more important matters. "So, Mr. Doyle, I'm like a fish out of water here. Obviously. May I borrow your phone to call my mother? I need to return home."

His heavy eyebrows lifted. "A phone, you say? What is a phone?"

"A smart phone? Cell phone? Telephone? You know, to make calls?" She almost snorted. This was peculiar beyond belief. Who hadn't heard of a phone?

Standing, he slapped his hands on the desk. "*Mademoiselle* Elaina, we do not have this 'phone' here at Wolfeshire Park. Come. The first order of business is to find you garments suitable for a fashionable coiffeuse. I shall turn you over to Mrs. Riddles' capable hands. She is the housekeeper; she will handle everything. After you are appropriately dressed, you shall have supper."

While Elaina *was* hungry, and her tummy certainly reminded her of that fact, she was absolutely floored by what the butler had said. It boggled the mind. No phone? No phone in the entire house? How in the world...?

She also stood and adjusted her blanket. "Where... I mean what country are we in, Mr. Doyle?"

"The King's country, *Mademoiselle* Elaina. England, of course. George IV is awaiting his coronation. But first the King is trying to get his unfortunate marriage dissolved."

Elaina opened her mouth but she couldn't speak. It felt as if all her circuits had gone on overload and had now been fried. George IV, also known as Prinny the Regent, had taken over the reins for the English monarchy for the very ill and failing George III from 1811 to 1820.

Mr. Doyle *couldn't* have been talking about George IV. After all, how could that be? But then again, George IV was who Mr. Doyle had mentioned.

As the man gently guided her out of the pantry and into the corridor, she could only blink. She'd had enough unpleasant surprises for the day. She needed to eat and then rest. Maybe if she slept, she'd awaken from this madness and everything would be normal again.

The butler stopped to talk with a stout, matronly woman who wore a somber black gown. Dangling from her waist was a grouping of chains holding an assortment of keys, a pair of scissors, a watch, household seals--metallic things that jingled when the woman walked.

Mr. Doyle and Mrs. Riddles chatted about proper clothing and nourishing food. Then he told the housekeeper that when *Mademoiselle* Elaina was ready, to send her to the nursery or Master Robert's bedchamber.

"*Mademoiselle* Elaina seems to be good for the boy," the butler commented. "She can calm him down. At least for the moment she can, at any rate."

Truth be told, while all this was going on, Elaina was still in a daze. Had she been drugged back in the park with Leila? Had someone whacked her on the head?

After Mr. Doyle gave her a pat on the shoulder, Elaina followed the housekeeper through a maze of narrow stairs and hallways. It took all of her focus, her energy, to do this simple act.

The reason for this was easy: her mind was churning over the impossible: had she really, honestly, truly, been transported back in time and over the ocean, and plopped down in George IV's England?

# Chapter Two

## 1820

Charles Robert Burnley, the eighth Duke of Wolfeshire, journeyed with his Wolfe Pack toward his ancestral home south of London in East Sussex. The distance from London to Wolfeshire Park was not far; by horseback it was a pleasant enough trip. The heat from the August sun however made the travel seem longer, more uncomfortable.

The saving grace here was that each member of the Pack were all glad to escape from the dubious charms of London in the summer: the rancid smells of the rotting city; the abnormally sweltering temperatures; and most of all, the circus-like atmosphere of Queen Caroline's trial now being held in the Parliamentary House of Lords.

Charles shuddered. Thank the good Lord that he had an excuse to escape that spectacle of vulgarity.

He glanced at the men riding by his sides and to his rear. His Pack usually consisted of seven elite members of the English haut ton, including himself. The men were all good company, but two of his set had recently succumbed to the parson's mousetrap, reducing the number to five.

Having bachelor status was *de rigueur* to obtain admittance into the Wolfe Pack. Charles himself had to abstain from his set's debauchery when he married eight years ago. His wife's unexpected death changed his status, freeing him to once again rule as leader of the Wolfe Pack.

Originally, the seven members of the Pack strove to be kings of one of the seven deadly categories of sin: pride, envy, gluttony, lust, anger, greed, and sloth.

Charles could claim "pride" for his own special sin. As a duke, the self-importance of that trait seemed particularly appropriate.

"Hold up, Wolfe," Lord Otto Blankton called out, maneuvering his trusty bronzed gelding next to Charles' gleaming stallion. "I know Wolfeshire Park is our destination however, I have to be frank, you must know I have one foot in dun territory. I cannot afford the, er, the expected tips to your servants for an extended stay."

Lord Otto's "sin" would be greed. Not that the man was acutely avaricious but as the third son of the Marquess of Haverham, Otto's fortunes were on the slim side. Marrying an heiress was in the wind for him, however he was in no hurry to give up his membership in the Wolfe Pack.

"Oh, for Heaven's sake," Alastair Dover, the new Earl of Nome, interrupted. He pulled in on the reins to slow his Arabian hot-blooded stallion. "Blankton, calm yourself. I'll sport the blunt for you."

Lord Nome's claim to the Wolfe Pack was lust--an excess of wenching, be it barmaids, actresses, members of the Fashionable Impure, or... other men's wives. Now that Alastair had just come into the title however, he was in need of finding his own wife. He would soon be dropping out of the Pack.

Then again, bets were on that Alastair would not be foregoing his wenching habits even with an exchange of wedding vows.

A plaintive voice came from behind the three of them. "I say, Wolfe, can we not stop at the next tavern? Y'know, to slake our thirst? Damme, this blasted August heat is making my tongue hang out. Rotters!"

The parched fellow bringing up the rear was Kenneth Martiz, Viscount Martiz. His "sin" was that of gluttony, in drink, food, and blowing a cloud. Then again, Kenneth had suffered a gunshot wound to the head during the war with the French. The miracle of it was that he survived; the unfortunate part about it was that one could never be sure what words would come out of his mouth, especially in mixed company.

Charles stopped his steed to discuss this change of plans. The rest of the Pack obliged him.

"A cold tankard does sound good. Up ahead in the next village, the Green Clover Tavern awaits us. Shall we stop? No more than one drink, agreed? We do not want to arrive at the Park three sheets in the wind."

The last of the Wolfe Pack, Mr. Jules Greensby, gave an unrestrained yawn. Greensby's sin was sloth. Plump as a baby with just as many fat folds, he was as indolent as a man could be. Rich as Croseus as the saying went, but just as sluggishly lazy.

"How much longer until we reach the Park, Wolfe? All this time on the road has made me fagged to death." Greensby finally remembered his manners and patted his yawning mouth with his chubby hand.

"Soon, Greensby. An hour at most."

Adjusting his tall beaver hat, Charles darted his gaze at his other friends. Suddenly, for some peculiar reason, the unaccustomed desire to be alone now consumed him. Right at this moment he would have given five hundred pounds for the solitary pleasure of being by himself.

Which was ironic since five hundred pounds was the penalty imposed upon peers of the realm for *not* attending the Queen's trial... unless they were excused. To be excused, a peer had to have been ill, was either too young or old, was in the bereavement period, practiced Roman Catholicism, or was away from England's shores.

And, not to forget, those peers who wavered on whether to attend the Queen's trial or not, the "incentive" of being imprisoned in the Tower of London was offered if one did not show up at the Parliamentary House of Lords.

Unconscionable.

Charles had avoided his so-called duty as a member of the House of Lords by claiming recent bereavement. However unfortunately, the bereavement was, indeed, true. His dear mother, Anastasia, the dowager duchess, had sighed her last sigh only one month ago, and he had to make suitable arrangements for the care of his son.

But, in addition to those duties, he now had to play the congenial host to his friends.

Devil take it! He was in no mood to entertain anyone, let alone these members of the Wolfe Pack. At the advanced age of three and thirty, he suddenly found he had no use for the sins of excess. Not anymore.

Excess. He had his fill of excesses.

Heading into the village ahead and the Green Clover Tavern, Charles shook his head to clear it. Visions of this morning's start of the formal proceedings against Caroline of Brunswick unfortunately filled his thoughts. The noise, the bawdy shouts, the pomp and circumstance...

Thursday, the seventeenth of August in this the year of our Lord 1820, would go down in the history books, but it would not be a day to be celebrated.

Sadly, no, it would not.

As Charles had made his excuses this morning to the Attendance Committee, he had viewed the heartbreaking figure of George IV who waited in the wings outside the trial chamber. The King visibly suffered from all the ravages of extreme excesses that he had subjected himself to over the years. The man was eight and fifty years; in appearance he resembled an infirm ninety-year-old.

Charles shuddered. Perhaps this morning's events were a personal warning to him. Perhaps Charles needed to mend his own ways with regards to excess.

"My dear girl," a schoolmarm-type of woman, dressed from head to foot in black, spoke softly. "Whyever are you dressed so... inappropriately?"

Situated in Mrs. Riddles sitting room, Elaina felt the heat of embarrassment creep up her cheeks. Her protective blanket had been removed and she stood before the housekeeper and the schoolmarm woman--Trundle, she was called--in her jeans and scooped-neck top. By the expressions on these two ladies' faces, one would have thought Elaina was naked.

But she wasn't, so she had no reason to feel self-conscious.

Unsettled would've been a better word to use. This sitting room's décor harkened back to days long since gone. Doilies, elaborate wooden furniture, fussy needlepoint, candlesticks... everything a person would expect to find in a nineteenth-century home.

The two women seated as Elaina modeled her twenty-first century clothing were both drenched in black. The only color came from the gleaming gold keys and whatnots dangling from the housekeeper's belt.

The other woman, probably forty or so, was, or rather had been, the personal maid of the lady of the house. As the lady in question was now deceased, the household all wore black for this period of mourning.

How many times did Elaina have to repeat her "story" to these people? Frankly, it was a wonder she could even function, given her completely bizarre circumstances.

She rubbed at her forehead. What had Trundle wanted to know? Oh yes, about her clothes. She'd better invent something... appropriate.

Right.

"It was the strangest thing. There I was, preparing to get dressed in my bedroom--"

"Bedchamber, dear," Mrs. Riddles corrected.

"Yes, bedchamber. Before I had a chance to put on my dress, I, um, I became dizzy. I must've fainted."

"What about your lady's maid, *Mademoiselle* Elaina? She should have helped you to your bed." Trundle made a tsk-tsk sound.

"Oh please, call me Elaina. I, um, sent the maid out to get a glass of water." She shrugged. "Anyway, I really don't know what happened next. Maybe I wandered outside? When I opened my eyes, I was here on the Park grounds. Robbie--"

"Master Robert," Mrs. Riddles corrected again.

"Um, yes. Master Robert found me and then showed me the way back to this house."

"The estate." Now the housekeeper indulged in a tsk-tsk. "How very odd. How very odd indeed." Then she smiled. "But you are not to worry, *Mademoiselle* Elaina. *Mademoiselle* Elaina is how we will refer to you. Never fear. We at Wolfeshire Park shall take care of you. We shall, indeed."

"Yes, indeed," Trundle chimed in. "The first item of business is to get *Mademoiselle* Elaina some appropriate clothes. Fannie, one of our housemaids, you know, will be bringing some of my dear mistress' fashionable garments for you to try on."

Trundle reached into a pocket hidden in the skirt of her long black gown and pulled out a cloth handkerchief. The handkerchief wasn't black, but a startling white. She dotted her eyes with it.

"As you have heard," Trundle sniffed, "the Dowager Duchess passed away last month, so very quickly into the shadow of death."

A duchess? How interesting. Robbie had mentioned that a duke lived at the Park. At the time she'd thought of the Dukes she knew--Jimmy and Nathan--but this estate belonged to an actual duke.

"My condolences," Elaina said solemnly. "This is very kind of you to help me and lend me clothes."

"Tush! 'Tis no trouble at all." Mrs. Riddles clapped her hands together. "I am sure the Dowager would have been most pleased with such a fine-looking gel like yourself, wearing her extensive wardrobe."

A knock sounded at the door. The housekeeper opened it to admit a young girl wearing a high-necked gown--also black--and a waisted white apron. She carried a three-quarter length sleeved gown in a medium color of grey.

"Beggin' yer pardon, ma'am. Here be one morning gown for *Mademoiselle* Elaina t'wear as we walk upstairs. I've got the remaining lot of Her Grace's gowns a-layin' on her bed. There are so many, I thought it best t'try 'em on in Her Grace's suite." The girl, Fannie, bobbed a curtsy.

She was a cute little thing, all pink-cheeked, slender, and mob-capped. Her sienna brown curls peeked out from under the cap. Elaina immediately liked her.

"Indeed. Excellent idea, Fannie. Excellent." Trundle jumped up and took the gown made of crinkled gauzy fabric. "Let me help you into this, *Mademoiselle* Elaina. I am assured the dress will fit you to perfection."

So, as modestly as she could, Elaina stripped off her jeans and blouse in front of three women. Fortunately Trundle quickly arranged the gown down over the shoulders and fastened the opening at the back.

Mrs. Riddles made a hefty sigh. "Pity the dress is not black but it will have to do for the nonce."

Fannie took a step forward. "The gown is French grey, so 'tis a half-mournin' color, ma'am."

"True, true," the housekeeper agreed. Then she and Trundle started talking about Elaina's next step, whatever the next step was.

By the wrinkles on both women's foreheads, Elaina knew they were worried.

But she wasn't. After all, to her, the worst had already happened: being separated from everyone she knew, from her home, her country, even from her own time. If that was even possible. How was her mother handling Elaina's evaporating into thin air? And Leila, had she been totally freaked out by the disappearance?

Elaina sighed. What about her full-service salon? Had that slipped through her fingers, too? Unless she could somehow duplicate the conditions responsible for hurling her through time, was she truly, honestly, irrevocably destined to remain in the past?

Oh boy, did she have a headache.

Mrs. Ripples pulled out a round timepiece hidden in one of her pockets. "Since the hour is advancing, we need to assign *Mademoiselle* Elaina a room of her own for the night. Until, of course, until things get settled."

Elaina placed her hand on the other woman's arm. "Please. If it can be arranged, can I share a room with one of your staff? I have a... fear of being alone, and this is a strange place for me. I know I wouldn't sleep a wink."

That much was true. Talk about being lost and totally vulnerable. She almost felt like a newborn, at everyone else's mercy.

Fannie piped up, "My room is clean and I have two beds; I use one as an extra dresser. I even have a window. I'd be honored t'share it with you, *Mademoiselle* Elaina." She blushed. "I don't snore, I promise. And I can also fix your hair. I've watched Trundle do the Dowager's."

Perfect! "I'd love to room with you! Thank you so much, Fannie."

That detail taken care of, Elaina said goodbye to Mrs. Ripples and went up the narrow staircase, heading for the Dowager Duchess' bedroom. Once the matter of the clothes was settled, she would be--according to Mr. Doyle--going to Robbie's room and having supper.

Thank goodness! She was as hungry as anything. And once that was done, her day would be through. Finally. She'd be able to sneak off to Fannie's room, get comfortable under the blanket, and close her eyes--tightly. She couldn't wait to shut out this very strange, peculiar, nineteenth-century world she now found herself in.

But for now, she had to hide her true identity from these people and play the part of a meek and mild French hairstylist, although maybe, in truth, she *was* one. After all her mother *was* half-French.

She sighed again.

Elaina glanced down at the finely-made Regency gown that had belonged to the Dowager Duchess. It fit her rather well, except for the over-spacious bust and the too-short length. Instead of the hem hitting the floor, the edge of the gown improperly ended by her anklebones.

How revealing! Definitely tongue-in-cheek!

If Elaina was going to stay here at Wolfeshire Park for any length of time--oh, please no!--she'd better rustle up a sewing needle and extra material fast so that she could lengthen these gowns. After all, she certainly didn't want to be "inappropriately" dressed!

**\* \* \* \***

Supper, dinner, whatever, was served in a cheery, blue, wallpapered room known as the nursery. As soon as Elaina stepped inside the toy-strewn room, Robbie dashed out from one of the doorways to stand before her. His bedroom, oops, bedchamber, must've been attached.

His dark hair combed into submission and his sky blue eyes focused on her, he marched over in his adult clothes: tailcoat, vest, and breeches. So very formal, and so very different from when she'd first met him!

He then actually bowed. "Elle, I'm happy to see you." Clapping his hands together, he crowed, "Ho! Finally we can eat. Are you starved?"

Since he bowed like a gentleman, she curtsied like a lady. "Absolutely starved, Robbie. The food smells wonderful. Thank you for inviting me."

He gestured to the small round table that held numerous silver platters and covered plates, along with expensive looking Wedgwood bone china.

She couldn't help being impressed. It must be nice to have the financial resources of a duke.

"Usually I have the footboy serve me, but tonight, I thought you could help me." He gave her a cheesy smile, revealing a missing front upper incisor. "I just want it to be you and me."

Interesting. She felt as if she had a seven-year-old suitor!

After they took their seats, she lifted the silver covers on the platter to reveal a cornucopia of fragrant offerings. Then she dished scoops of food onto his plate.

He popped a black olive into his mouth. "Good-O! Roasted chicken and ham pie is one of my favorites. You'll like it too, Elle."

An enthusiastic eater was always good company. She smiled. "I'm sure I will. It smells yummy."

"Yummy! I like that." Robbie tittered. "It smells yummy. I'm going to tell Cook her food is *yummy*."

Elaina adjusted her position in the child-sized chair and then buttered one of the obviously homemade rolls. "I have to thank you, Robbie, for helping me today. For inviting me to your house and for this dinner. Honestly, I don't know what I would've done if you hadn't come along."

Lowering his gaze, he seemed to find his silver fork fascinating. His dark eyelashes were so long and thick; for a moment she envied him.

Then he looked over at her. "It was meant to be, Elle. I mean, I made a wish for... well, for something, and then I found you. I'm going to keep you, I don't care what Doyle or my father says."

*Keep me?*

She had to contain her laugh so she took a sip of overly sweet lemonade. "Truthfully, Robbie, I'm not a possession like these toy soldiers you've decorated the floor with. Nobody is a possession. I'm a person; you can't keep me. I don't belong to you. I don't belong to anyone really, but believe me I'm very thankful to--"

"No!" His gorgeous blue eyes narrowed and almost shot out sparks. "You are mine and I'm keeping you here. You're going to stay with me and sleep in my bed."

Oh! How very... *inappropriate!*

Robbie was an extremely strong-willed boy. She didn't have much experience with children--being an only child and all--but she knew she had to nip his bad behavior in the bud.

She folded her hands in front of her on the table. "Robbie, that's not going to happen. It's not... well, to use Ms.... um, Trundle's word... it's not appropriate for members of the opposite sex to, um, sleep in the same room."

"Stuff!" He pushed away from the table and stood. *"I'm* the master of Wolfeshire Park, at least I am when my father is away, so what I say, goes."

Pointing his small index finger at her he crinkled up his non-angelic face. "And I want you with me always."

Always? She bit her lip. This dear little boy must've been missing his mother. Where was she?

"No, Robbie. Besides, I've got arrangements to stay with Fannie for the night. She was kind enough to invite me to use her spare bed."

"Fannie? Fannie?" He stomped around the parquet flooring and kicked his toy soldiers out of his way. "She's just a servant. She cleans the rooms. Stay with me and I'll take care of you."

As if his word was indeed law, he thumped on his meager chest.

Temper tantrums. Hmmn. Elaina dotted her lips with her napkin and then placed it on the table. She'd better stage a quick exit.

Taking a deep breath, she said calmly, "This dinner is over. I need to go."

"No!" Holding his hand out, Robbie rushed over to stop her from rising. "No. If you don't want to sleep in my bed, I'll have another one brought in so we can be side by side. I won't crowd you, Elle. Promise."

She now huffed out an exasperated breath. What could she do, what could she say to calm Robbie down?

"Besides, Elle, it'll be acceptable. I'm a little boy, not a man." He shuffled his leather-clad foot on the floor. "Maybe you can be my new mother."

Whoa! Elaina shot up out of the chair. Then she got on one knee in front of him so she could be on the same level and look him right in the eye.

"What happened to your mother, Robbie?"

"She died. Two years ago." He sniffed. "And then, and then, my grandmother passed away last month."

"Oh, I'm so sorry Robbie. But as for being your new mother, that's impossible. Besides, I don't know anything about little boys... or about being a mother. And for that matter, I know absolutely nothing about dukes."

She curved her arm around his slender shoulders. "Let's forget about all that, okay? Why don't we play some games until bedtime? And then, after you get cleaned up for bed, I'll read you a story."

He blinked his watery eyes. "Two?"

"Sure. Two stories."

"Will you sing to me? My mama always did."

Elaina leaned over to kiss the top of his head. "You drive a hard bargain. I'm sure your mother had a better voice, but okay, I'll give it a go. Just don't complain!"

Nodding his head, he sniffed, so she pulled one of the ubiquitous handkerchiefs from the pocket in his breeches, then handed it to him.

"Thank you," he spoke softly.

How sweet. Her heart did a little jump in her chest.

Standing, she walked them both over to a shelving unit loaded with blocks, balls, books, spinning tops, something that looked like Pick Up Sticks, and enough toy soldiers on horseback to win a war.

With the back of his hand, he swept the toy figures onto the ground. "Let's play with these." He plopped down on the floor. "I like to sit and play."

Pulling up her gown to her knees, she sat cross-legged on the floor. "I do too! C'mon, let's get started."

His brows met at the bridge of his adorable nose. "I'll be the red Royal Dragoons and you can be the French."

"Naturally. They don't call me *Mademoiselle* for nothing, right?"

Robbie nodded with approval. "Good-O! And when we're finished, we can have one of Cook's special Fig and Apple Tarts... right?"

She smiled. "Sounds yummy!"

"Yummy! Let's play, Elle."

As strange as it seemed, Elaina's first night back in the nineteen-century consisted of playing on the losing side of the Napoleonic War with Bonaparte's grenadiers of the French Imperial Guards. But no matter. She honestly wouldn't have thought it possible, but she really was enjoying herself... and the company.

# Chapter Three

The first order of business for Charles after the vigorous journey from London was a relaxing bath to remove travel dirt. Most likely, his Pack would follow suit. Soon they would all be dressed to perfection and meet downstairs in the Gold Drawing Room to then move into the Grand Dining Room for supper. At the mahogany table designed by Thomas Chippendale, they would dine on sumptuous delicacies as prepared by Charles' cook, Mrs. Parsons.

He had not given advanced notice to his staff that he would be entertaining four gentlemen until Monday, however butler Doyle and housekeeper Mrs. Ripples could and did handle any circumstances thrown their way.

The dinner would be exceptional; Charles was assured of that.

Afterwards, the Pack would settle in to play a card game or two. Whist? Speculation? Cassino? Who knew? The game was of little importance. In the Gold Drawing Room there would be drinking and smoking cheroots and idle banter.

An exorbitant amount of idle banter. And with that thought, Charles sighed.

Once clean and dry, he allowed his trusty valet, Wilkins, to help him into his evening clothes. Nothing pretentious, after all it was only Thursday night, however black was the color of the night. No surprise there since Wolfeshire Park was in mourning. Black wool tailcoat, waistcoat, breeches, stockings, and satin pumps. The only other colors were shiny silver for his tailcoat's front buttons, and the stark white of his shirt and cravat.

Before taking the grand staircase down to the Gold Drawing Room, he stopped with his hand on the elaborately carved banister. He could admit to feeling uneasy. On edge. Disturbed. This apprehensive feeling had to do with his son.

Usually when Charles returned to Wolfeshire Park, his son made a spectacle of himself by stomping his foot and insisting to see his father--immediately. With his grandmother now gone, and of course, his mother as well, gone these two years, Robert had a tendency to run wild. He was the main reason Charles had rushed home to provide some stability in his misbehaving son's life.

However, as yet, Robert had not made an appearance. Unusual. Most unusual, indeed.

Turning from the staircase, Charles headed for his son's bedchamber to check up on him. He found his son not in his bedchamber but the nursery, preparing to eat.

Seated with him at the small table was, of all things, an attractive young woman. Very young and fresh faced. Her vivid brown hair was pulled up into a bun with a riot of curls framing her forehead. Her pink lips appeared natural, untouched by artificial salve.

Who the devil was she? She had an unforgettable face. He was certain he had never seen her before.

What she wore, however, he *had* seen. This grey gown--French grey he believed it was called--had been one of his mother's favorites for the morning hours. So why the devil was this girl wearing it? Who gave her permission? It was a certainty he would be speaking with his mother's lady's maid, Trundle, in the very near future.

His son smiled at the girl, revealing his missing tooth. Well-behaved, Robert stated that he wanted only the two of them in the nursery. Him and her.

Blast! If the boy had numbered more than seven to his years, Charles would have been truly alarmed. But Robert was only a child; Charles did not have to be concerned about... the boy chasing after buxom maids for at least a little while longer.

About to interrupt this *tête-à-tête* of his son's, Charles paused to listen to their conversation. Oftentimes, more could be learned by eavesdropping instead of barging in.

The boy called her "Elle" and repeated her interesting word--yummy. Yummy was a word Charles had never heard before either.

She very politely thanked Robert for his help.

Charles rubbed his chin. What on God's good Earth did Robert help her with? Was she taking advantage of his son's kind nature?

Then he heard her call the boy "Robbie." Charles saw red. He flared his nostrils. No one called the son of a duke, "Robbie."

Straightening up from resting against the nursery door, Charles heard something else. Something even more outrageous. Robert then stated he was going to keep her, despite what others, like his father, said!

That could not be condoned. Charles took a step inside, but then the woman's response stopped him cold.

*"I'm not a possession like these toy soldiers you have decorated the floor with. Nobody is a possession. I'm a person; you can't keep me. I don't belong to you."*

Charles stared at the girl's back in astonishment. How had this... this person gotten so wise?

Then, when Robert talked about them both sleeping in the same bed, the girl very calmly turned him down.

*"That's not going to happen. It's not... well, to use Ms.... um, Trundle's word... it's not appropriate for members of the opposite sex to, um, sleep in the same room."*

Then she continued:

*"Besides, I've got arrangements to stay with Fannie for the night. She was kind enough to invite me to use her spare bed."*

Fannie was one of the housemaids. What the devil was going on at Wolfeshire Park behind Charles' back?

He almost choked on hearing Robert's next sentence. "Maybe you can be my new mother."

This girl was not at a loss for words, though.

*"No, Robbie, that's impossible. Besides, I don't know anything about little boys... or about being a mother. And for that matter, I know absolutely nothing about dukes."*

Charles frowned. Any female in his acquaintance would have jumped at the chance to become a duchess. *His* duchess even more so. But not this girl, this Elle. Not that she could ever hope to fill the duchess' high position. The very idea was impossible.

*Who the devil is she?*

After the pair of them decided to play with toy soldiers, they sat cross-legged on the floor as if they both had been born to that position.

Charles backed away from the nursery. He would not confront the girl, not until he knew more about this unusual situation.

He headed for the staircase. Soon the dinner gong would ring and he needed to greet his guests as they entered the Gold Drawing Room.

He certainly had a great deal to think about. In addition, he had a few of his household staff to question, namely, lady's maid Trundle, housemaid Fannie, housekeeper Mrs. Riddles, butler Doyle, and Robert's nanny Price.

Nothing happened at Wolfeshire Park without the butler and the housekeeper knowing. One way or the other, Charles would find out exactly what was going on with this Elle and his precocious young son.

* * * *

"I say, Wolfe, dinner was excellent. Top-of-the-tree, top-of-the-line, top-dog, what?" Patting his extended stomach, Jules Greensby made himself comfortable by slumping down on the elongated, carved settee designed by Robert Adam.

The four other members of the Pack also relaxed in the cosy chairs arranged around the Gold Drawing Room's white alabaster fireplace. A drink of choice in one hand and a handcrafted cigar in the other, the gentlemen were doing as Charles had predicted: indulging in idle banter.

"Stap me!" Greensby continued. "I look forward to tomorrow night's meal... and Saturday's."

Alastair Dover, Lord Nome, sat to Greensby's right, not only slumped down but with one leg inelegantly swinging over the arm on the wing-backed chair. "Food. Is that all you think about, Greensby? After all, as it is written in the bible, Matthew 4:4, I believe, 'Man shall not live on bread alone.'"

Greensby's doughy face reddened. "Just making conversation, Alastair. I've a right to enjoy my dinner."

"You enjoy it too much," Nome drawled. "Besides, you need to address me as 'Nome'. *I've* a right to enjoy my new inheritance."

Once again Charles regretted his decision to gather the Pack at Wolfeshire Park. An entire evening together had not yet passed, and at least two of them were growling at each other's throats.

"Peace, good fellows." Charles lifted a decanter of fine, aged whisky, ready to replenish those who desired a refill. "Let us not tear into each other. We are all fortunate to have escaped our so-called duty to the Crown. Your coming into the earldom, Alastair, is a very recent occurrence. Sometimes I shall call you that, and sometimes 'Nome.' It is of little import. However, the fact that your uncle died did you another service. You were able to avoid the Queen's trial as did I on the bereavement issue."

Nome raised his glass for a top off. "I concede. Sorry, Greensby. After all, you're only doing what you're supposed to as the Pack's ambassador of gluttony."

Seated on the same settee as Greensby, but at the other end, Kenneth, Lord Martiz, shook his curly-haired head. "No, no, you've got it wrong, Nome. *I'm* the god-dammed emissary of gluttony, hey? After all, this is my fifth glass of scotch whisky."

He flung his left arm in Greensby's direction, thereby spilling some of the amber liquid onto the settee's floral cushions. "Greensby here is our representative of laziness, hey?"

Greensby bobbed his thickset head. "Much obliged to you, Martiz."

Nome sat up straight and leaned toward the settee. "I admit to curiosity. How did you escape the mandatory attendance of the trial, Martiz? You're a peer of the realm. Why didn't they lock you up in the Tower?"

Martiz smoothed his hand over the side of his head. His curls covered the site of his bullet wound. "Odd's life, that's easy. My situation fit under the 'illness' category. And just to seal the deal, I purposefully threw a slew of salty language at the Attendance Committee. Swore like a damn bloody sailor, I believe is the description."

Raucous laughter filled the Gold Drawing Room, along with fresh cigar smoke.

Picking up the whisky decanter, Nome then walked over to Martiz and refilled his glass. "Continue on with your gluttony, Martiz."

"Here, h-here!" hiccupped Lord Otto Blankton as he leaned over to his side table and dumped his cigar ashes into a tray. "I've got a capital idea: let us indulge ourselves in a game or two of whist."

Nome threw back his head and laughed. "Trying to win some blunt, eh? You poor, and I do mean *poor,* bastard. Tell us, how did you escape the Parliament's decree?"

Blankton shrugged his slender shoulders. "No mystery there, Nome. I'm not a member of the House of Lords--not yet, at any rate. I've got my father, the Marquess, and two older brothers ahead of me."

Martiz piped up, "What about you, Greensby? You're rich enough for ten men. How'd you avoid getting pulled into the trial?"

"Easy enough." Greensby grinned. "I'm a plain mister, don't you know. Not a peer but a commoner."

Charles stood. They all had ruminated long enough. He snapped his fingers for a footman and ordered, "Set up a card table in here."

Then he turned to his Pack. "So, as you know, the game of whist requires four players, not five. What I propose is this: the first round of whist, I shall partner with Nome, while Blankton and Greensby will also partner up. This allows you, Martiz, to recover from your... inebriation."

Martiz slowly nodded. "My thanks, Wolfe. I do feel a damned bit muzzle-headed."

Charles nodded back. "For the next round, Martiz will take my place. Are we agreed?"

Four vigorous bellows of "agreed" echoed off the Gold Drawing Room's four walls.

Now prepared to concentrate on the trumps and tricks of whist, Charles allowed his mind to wander. He had consciously decided to wait until tomorrow to question his staff about the mysterious girl upstairs. After all, tomorrow morning would be just as good as tonight, and frankly there was not much he could do about the situation at this advanced hour. Perhaps, after his round of whist, he would bid his friends goodnight and then look in on his son to see that Robert was safely abed.

If Charles happened to run into the girl, then... then he would...

Hell. His imagination failed him. He had no idea of what he would do if he did happen to see her.

**\* \* \* \***

In Robbie's nighttime-dark bedroom, Elaina turned up the lever on the oil lamp, which then illuminated the area by the bed with bright yellow light.

"There," she said to the little boy huddled into her as she leaned up against the wooden headboard on the very high mattress. "Now I can see better."

"Read me another." Robbie huffed a great sigh. "You promised me another."

The dear boy was fighting to stay awake. His rosebud lips pouted, his thick eyelashes fluttered, his breathing rate deepened, but still he remained awake.

If anything should've put him to sleep, it was the last book she'd read: *The Good Child's Illustrated Alphabet.* That was more of a lesson on letters, more appropriate for the day than a nighttime story.

It started with: A was an Archer, who shot at a frog. B was a Butcher, and kept a great dog. C was a Captain, all covered with lace... all the way through to Z was a Zany, a silly old fool.

"Another one," Robbie insisted as he snuggled into the side of her hip with his eyes half closed. "You promised."

What a sweet boy. She smoothed her hand through his tumble of curls. He had a cheery room, and now she could see it better in the light. It was wallpapered with posies of flowers. Next to the fireplace was a washer stand complete with towels and a pitcher and bowl in a flowered ceramic for morning clean up. On the floor was one of those chamber pots, also in a flowered design.

Scattered about the room were small wooden chairs that she herself had outgrown many years ago. Covering the floor was a, no doubt, expensive Aubusson carpet, made chiefly for aristocrats--who else would have that kind of money?

Yep, little Robbie was rich, and his bed was very large for a child. It could've accommodated two, as he had told her, however she certainly wasn't going to take him up on his offer! The headboard and footboard were made of dark English walnut, carved with fancy scrolls and decorations.

A fringed white bedspread served double duty: as a cover for a made-up bed and also a blanket for the night. Lying across the bottom was a beautifully made quilt composed of different colored octagonal shapes.

To the side of the bed was one of those bed step stools. The mattress was so high off the floor, Robbie needed this to get up and then step down. But, if he slept too close to the edge of the mattress and then turned...

Ouch. Elaina shivered.

Nothing really stood out as this bedroom being a child's room except for a long-legged, stuffed teddy bear resting against the bed pillows. Robbie now nestled this teddy under his arm.

As most of the children's books in his nursery were a little bizarre for twenty-first century tastes, like the title, *The Tragical Death Of An Apple Pie,* also featuring the alphabet, she offered an alternative.

"How about if I tell you the story of one of my favorite fairytales. It's about a valiant tailor who boasted he killed seven at one blow. Everyone assumed he killed seven men at a stroke, but that wasn't it. Do you know what the tailor was talking about?"

Robbie shook his tired head. "No, I don't, Elle. What was it?"

"Flies!" She clapped her hands.

As tired as he was, Robbie giggled.

"So let me tell you the tailor's story." Elaina began and then shortened the adventures to end up with the tailor vanquishing his foes and marrying the princess.

By this time Robbie was breathing deeply, and frankly she was too. She was more than ready to hit the bed and put an end to this absolutely crazy day.

As quietly as she could, she slipped out from under the boy's tight grasp.

"Sing." He fluttered his eyes open. "Mama sings."

Oh boy. Elaina nibbled on her lower lip. "I don't really know a lullaby."

"Sing," he softly sighed.

One more minute and he'd be out. She cleared her throat and sang the first thing that popped up in her mind.

"You are my sunshine, my only sunshine

You make me happy when skies are grey

You'll never know dear, how much I love you

Please don't take my sunshine away." [1]

Ah! He fell asleep! Brushing aside the hair hanging down on his forehead, she placed a brief kiss there.

"Sleep tight, Robbie."

She scooted off the high bed, turned down the oil lamp, and then took one of the beeswax candles lighting the mantel on the fireplace to help her find her way in this huge house.

Goodness, she never felt as exhausted as she did right now. Then again, maybe she had but she'd forgotten the experience. The only thing she knew for sure was that she'd never been back in the nineteenth century! Now if only she could remember how to get to the servants' side of this humongous place.

Carefully walking to the small corridor that led to the exit door, Elaina gasped. Someone grabbed her upper arm.

"Oh!" In the darkness, the mellow flame of the candle wavered in the breeze, revealing the ghostly illumination of a tall man's face.

"W-Who are you?" she stammered.

"No, m'dear." The man's deep voice scared her and thrilled her at the same time. "The more pertinent question is, who the devil are *you?*"

1. "You Are My Sunshine", published by Jimmie Davis and Charles Mitchell, 1940.

# Chapter Four

Charles pulled the interloper out into the hallway. She was a pretty filly, he would give her that, however no one, *no one* had access to his son that he--Charles--had not first approved of.

Looking down into her brown ringed with green eyes, he tightened his hold on her upper arm. "I repeat, who the devil are you?"

The girl had the audacity to look down her nose at him. "Unhand me, sir!"

And then she spoiled the severe effect by grinning. "Oh, I've always wanted to use that line. So dramatic."

His nostrils flared. He waited for her to come to her senses.

Finally, she did. "Okay, you don't look amused. So, obviously, you don't know me. My name is Elaina Wattell." She ran her gaze over him, lingering on his face. "I'm assuming your Robbie's father?"

"His name is Robert, you brazen-faced baggage."

He watched her lower lip tremble, then she lifted her hand so that the candle was higher. Now her face was as equally lit as was his.

"I don't even know what a brazen-faced baggage means. But listen, can we sort this all out tomorrow? I'm, well, truthfully, I'm exhausted. I feel like I'd give my right kidney for a good night's sleep." After staring at him, she then lowered her gaze and mumbled, "Changing centuries is no way to spend a birthday."

Who in God's name was this girl? Her dark hair gleamed in the candlelight, her smooth complexion showed no signs of ravishes--not by time, disposition, nor chemically harsh cosmetic coverings. She appeared to advantage in his mother's simple day gown, however the inadequate length revealed a comely set of ankles. She had a peculiar accent and a very odd way with her words.

He yanked on her captured arm. "I will have my answers now."

Her lips extended mulishly. "I'm an American. I come from New York, and that is, as you know, very far away. I'm a hairstylist, what you might call a coiffeuse."

Then, suddenly, she yawned. This girl, this Elaina Wattell, had the presence of mind to cover her yawning mouth with her hand, even though he still maintained his grip on her arm. She had more manners than Jules Greensby.

"Sorry," she murmured. "But I did tell you I'm bushed. It's been quite a day."

She seemed to be unsteady on her feet. Charles glanced around the darkened corridor but did not find what he was seeking: a chair or bench for this girl to rest on. Traveling down the grand staircase was out of the question; in the condition she was in, she would not be able to navigate the steps. Plus, if any of his Pack, especially Nome, saw her, then her dubious virtue might very well be assaulted.

No, he would take her to the sitting room in his bedchamber suite.

"Come with me." He tugged on her arm and walked toward his sitting room. "You may sit and then answer my questions."

She almost tripped on her own feet. "But why can't we wait until tomorrow? Honestly, the way I feel right now I might just drop off to sleep standing on my feet."

He wanted to smile; he found her complaining to be amusing, but he kept a stern face. "Just another minute and you can sit on the settee. Here."

He opened the door into the sitting room. Fortunately the room was already lit with candles and oil lamps.

She stepped inside and then headed straight for the satin striped settee.

"Nice." With that word, she sat, set her head on the back cushion, and closed her eyes.

"No." He leaned over and shook her shoulder. "You are not to sleep here."

She was not listening to him. Moving as sensuously as any woman he had known in his acquaintance, she wiggled her way to a more comfortable spot.

"Too bad I can't lie down," she huffed.

He pulled a chair closer to her position and then sat in front of her. "No... Miss Wattell, is it? No, you are not to lie down. You are to answer my questions. All of them. Why are you here?"

She flashed her eyes at him. They now appeared more brown than green. "I don't know why. Have you heard of hypnosis? My girlfriend wanted to try it on me, so she did. I closed my eyes and then I woke up in the woods. Your woods. Your son... such a cute little boy... he found me and brought me here."

Her chest rose and fell so peacefully. She closed her eyes once again. "Please, let me sleep. That's all there is to the story. Promise."

He had to shake his head in disbelief. Here this female was, in the presence of a duke, and all she wanted of him was to allow her to sleep? Preposterous!

"You mentioned centuries, Miss Wattell. And a birthday. Whose birthday?"

She snuggled in against the back squabs. "My birthday. I'm twenty-four. Happy birthday to me. Ha."

"Who gave you permission to play with my son? To read to him? Sing to him? And even dare to kiss his forehead? What manner of female are you?"

"I'm a tired female. And you'd be too if you'd... well, never mind." She glanced over at him. "Not that you'd be a female. I just meant being tired."

"Why are you wearing the Dowager's clothes?"

She took a deep breath. "I don't have anything else to wear here. No joke. Please let me..."

Her eyes fluttered closed again, but this time she was honest and truly gone to the land of Morpheus.

Jumping out of his chair, Charles paced. Sometimes activity helped his thoughts. What on God's green Earth should he do with this girl... this woman?

Should he make her comfortable on the settee? Should he move her to his bed? Should he join her?

Begad! Was a man ever as bedeviled as he?

He heard a soft knock at his door. Being a careful man, he asked, "Yes?"

"Your Grace, Doyle here."

Doyle! A good man. A good butler. He would know the best course of action.

"Come." Charles waited until the butler closed the door and then stood next to him. "Tell me, Doyle, how do you explain this?"

He dramatically extended his arm in the sleeping woman's direction. "You see I am in a devil of a coil. How on God's good Earth did this woman get here?"

"Sir," Doyle inclined his majestic head. "As I understand the matter, Master Robert found *Mademoiselle* Elaina on the grounds. That is what Mrs. Riddles and I have been calling her, since she says she is a coiffeuse."

Charles nodded. "Yes, the woman mentioned that." He strode over to the sideboard and poured himself another whisky. "I am quite out of humour with this situation, I can tell you. The House of Wolfeshire is in mourning, blast it. The Dowager Duchess passed just one month ago. And now here... here is a problematic woman with uncertain morals."

He turned and faced the butler. "This female had the audacity to say that she wore my mother's gown because she did not have anything else to wear."

Doyle's ruddy tone pinkened. "Sir, I believe *Mademoiselle* Elaina is a harmless stray. Master Robert seems quite taken with her. Indeed, his behavior has much improved since being in her company."

"The company of a questionable waif? I do not have words..." Charles continued his pacing, looking at the woman's sleeping form as he passed her. Her head had fallen back to rest upon the wall, exposing the long line of her supple neck--a neck made for worshipping. For kissing...

He shut his eyes for a moment. May the good Lord help him, he had not had a woman in too long a time.

"What the devil am I to do with her?" he said more to himself than to his butler.

Doyle cleared his throat. "Your Grace, she might make a tolerable governess for Master Robert."

The woman murmured and moved her head to the side, exposing the luscious skin behind her ear.

The devil! Charles fisted his hands.

"A governess? This piece of baggage can barely speak the King's English!"

"It was only a suggestion, sir. She does seem to be knowledgeable in many areas. You might want to discuss her qualifications with her on the morrow."

Finishing his drink, Charles set the glass down on the sideboard. "What about now? What shall be done with her for the rest of the night? Should she remain here?"

For some reason, that very thought excited him.

"Begging your pardon, sir. Mrs. Riddles and I have already made arrangements for *Mademoiselle* Elaina to room with the housemaid Fannie."

Charles feasted on the woman's relaxed form. The neckline on the gown gapped open on one side to reveal more succulent flesh.

He ran his tongue over his lips. "Perhaps the woman should have her own room."

Doyle cleared his throat again. "Very kind of you to suggest, sir, however, *Mademoiselle* Elaina specifically asked to room with one of our maids. She states she has a fear of being alone, and considering her circumstances, she will feel more comfortable with the arrangement already made."

Exhaling a deep breath, Charles agreed with his butler. "Yes. Good. She looks uncomfortable with her neck stretched as it is. I shall carry her up to the maid's room."

"Sir." Doyle held out his beefy hand, close to, but not touching Charles' upper arm. "Begging your pardon, but that would not be prudent. The Duke of Wolfeshire carrying a female into the servant quarters, if seen, would generate an avalanche of gossip. In addition, *Mademoiselle* Elaina's reputation would be thoroughly disparaged."

Charles blinked. "Yes, yes. What was I thinking?" He rubbed at his alcohol-blurred mind to calm his thoughts. "Yes, of course. So we should wake her up then?"

"No need, Your Grace. I trust *Mademoiselle* Elaina is as light as thistledown. I will carry this hapless chit up to the servants' quarters where, without a doubt, Fannie is already in her room for the night."

Although Charles truly hated to see another man carry the unconscious Elaina Wattell, he supposed it was for the best. He did not trust his inebriated self, but he did trust Doyle with this dainty package. How peculiar that he felt that way.

He watched as Doyle slid one arm under her knees and then lifted her up to rest against his chest. The woman's head lolled against the butler, and at the intimate sight Charles fisted his hands again.

He followed Doyle out into the corridor and to where the servants' stairs were hidden. After opening the door, he called to the butler. "Leave instructions for the woman to come to my Library in the morning. At eleven o'clock, that should be late enough for her."

"Yes, Your Grace," Doyle said as he carried the precious bundle up the winding stairs.

Charles stood at the doorway threshold, listening to the vanishing sounds of the butler's footsteps. Once the steps had faded, with a sigh, Charles turned and went back to his bedchamber. Not only did his suite feel emptier than it had just moments before, but he felt emptier as well.

Blast! What he needed was a good night's sleep to restore his equilibrium.

✳ ✳ ✳ ✳

Usually when Elaina woke from her sleep, she was, to use a phrase, bright-eyed and bushy-tailed. Today wasn't one of those days.

Everything that could ache on her body ached with a vengeance. What in the world had she done to merit such unmitigated pain? As her mother would always say, she felt like a Mack truck had run over her.

The answer came to Elaina in a resounding flash. Time-travel. She'd somehow landed over two hundred years back... back in the past.

Afraid to open her eyes, she bit on her lower lip. Was it possible that she'd just had a nightmare?

In her heart she knew the truth of the matter. No, what she'd experienced yesterday was real. All her senses confirmed that she no longer resided in the twenty-first century.

Ooh. A chill of gigantic proportions shook her out of any lingering drowsiness.

The smell of the air was different. It was a cleaner, fresher scent imbued with flowers but, perhaps a bit of musty mold, also.

The sounds she heard seemed to hum sweeter--song birds chirping outside, singing about the glorious new day; the rush of movement coming from beyond this bedroom; the creaking and groaning of the wood flooring all contributed to a symphony of a simpler life.

The feel of harsh, stiff starch on her skin from the sheets on this bed and the thin cotton on her blanket covering were all different from the sensations she usually woke up to.

As for taste... her mouth felt less dry as was usual. She had no cottonmouth this morning.

Which left sight. She had to be brave and confront this strange new world head-on.

With a sigh, she sat up in bed and took a look at her surroundings. Her twin bed with a metal railing headboard was pushed against a wall. The other bed was on the farther wall, made up nice and neatly for the day.

Sunlight entered the one window in between the beds. It probably wasn't early; she'd probably overslept.

She noticed she was wearing a thin cotton nightgown. Fannie must've helped her into it because she had no memories of anything other than...

A man. A very impressive and, by the smell of whisky, an intoxicated man.

Yes, that had been Robbie's father. He'd spoken to her. He wanted answers, and goodness, she'd been so out of it, she didn't remember what she told him.

She did remember how handsome he was. His dark hair a curly mop like his son's, broad shoulders and well-formed thighs... and thick lips that were made for kissing. And his eyes, what color were his eyes?

Blacker than the darkest black.

She sighed. Yesterday, back with Leila, when Elaina had focused on what she wanted, what she needed to heal herself--wishing for a duke-- she certainly hadn't meant *him,* Robbie's father. After all, she hadn't even met him, and she didn't even know his name.

A rattle sounded at the doorknob and in hurried a crisply dressed Fannie, with her short-sleeved gown and glaringly white long apron.

"Good mornin'! I be so glad you're awake. Why, I never did see anyone as tired as you last night. Do you feel ever so much better today?"

"Yes, I do. Thanks, Fannie, for all your help. I certainly don't remember getting up here and changing into this nightgown."

"Such goings on, for sure! Do y'know, Mr. Doyle himself carried you here? Such a strong one, he is." She patted at her heart.

Elaina felt her face heat up. "Oh, no, I don't remember that."

"Well, never mind. You've got t'get a move on now, girl. You've just enough time t'get yourself ready. Mr. Doyle says you're expected in the Library at eleven. T'see the Duke, no less!"

"The Duke?" Elaina swallowed down her surprise. What did he want to see her for? He hadn't been a happy camper yesterday. Was he going to kick her out?

No. No. No.

Ooh. She rubbed on her forehead. If he did, then where would she go? Where *could* she go? She needed time to figure out how she could reverse this... this curse so she could go back to where she came from.

Fannie came over to Elaina's bed and helped her to her feet. "Now, no worries. I can get you freshened up and dressed in no time at all. I'll even do your hair again." She gave a tinkle of a giggle. "I be your lady's maid, *Mademoiselle* Elaina! At least for today."

"Just Elaina, okay, Fannie? But first, I need to, um, use the chamber pot."

Oh, to have a regular bathroom! That was what she probably missed the most!

Fannie gave her a wink. "I leave you be, then. I be right outside. Open the door when you're ready."

Elaina nodded. A gazillion thoughts swirled around in her brain. She instinctively knew she had to be at her best. Her future... in the past... depended on it.

**\* \* \* \***

As Charles sat behind his massive mahogany desk, he rifled through legal papers concerning his mother's death. Since no one else was in the Library, there was no need to sit ramrod straight; he allowed his shoulders to slump. He had a devil of a head from last night's dissipation.

Drinking to excess was Kenneth Martiz's claim to fame, not Charles'.

He took a sip of lukewarm tea, and then set the delicate cup back in its saucer. He sighed. Why the devil was he so on edge?

His desk clock ticked on: fifteen minutes before the hour of eleven. Each tick seemed to disturb him further. At eleven o'clock, his unexpected "guest" was due to walk through the Library's solid oak doors.

Blast it! What the devil was he going to do about that girl, that woman Elaina Wattell?

A bubbly warble from a common house wren filtered in through the floor-to-ceiling window to the right of his desk. He watched the bird jump from tree branch to tree branch. The chirpy song was cheery, uplifting, full of life as if to remind him that instead of sinking into the dismals, he should take a deep breath and enjoy what he had.

He did have a vast amount to enjoy, he had to admit that. Naturally, he had duties and responsibilities, however he also could indulge himself in spontaneous pleasures, as he had in inviting his Pack to Wolfeshire Park.

For example, this afternoon he and his Pack would participate in a walking shoot of red grouse so plentiful on his estate. His specially trained dogs, not foxhounds, would be delighted for the exercise and the excitement to flush the beggars out. As was usual, the game would then be distributed among tenants on the estate. Waste not, want not.

And after dinner, perhaps the Pack would enjoy another round of whist. It was to be hoped Lord Otto's empty coffers had received an infusion last night.

Tomorrow, Saturday, starting at eleven, there would be a small-scale foxhunt. Nothing official, more like a practice run. The hunt would consist of just him and his Pack readying themselves for the season that would start in November.

For Saturday's evening hours, an informal gathering with a few neighbors would tolerably pass the time. After dinner, they all would indulge in country dancing and perhaps a game of charades.

Sunday, of course, would be a day of rest. There would be church services, and the mandatory Sunday lunch of roast beef. Perhaps, afterwards if the afternoon rains held off, there could be some long walks, or the solitary pleasure of a good book or catching up on world events via newspapers.

And Monday, perhaps the day Charles was looking forward to the most, his Pack would leave.

A frown pulled down his lips. But then again, that brought him full circle. What the devil was he going to do about Elaina Wattell?

Before he had an answer to his dilemma, a knock sounded on the Library door.

It was her. It had to have been her.

Charles' gaze riveted on the door and his breath hitched. "Come."

Doyle's black-clad arm opened the door and he inserted his head inside the Library. "Your Grace, *Mademoiselle* Elaina to see you as you requested."

Everything stood still in that moment. In walked a goddess of youth and beauty. Charles could not react, even if he had wanted to. Everything about Elaina Wattell was pleasing: the woman's dark hair very suitably arranged, her complexion smooth and fresh, her lips naturally pink and full...

Of course he recognized the morning gown she wore. Or rather mourning gown. His mother had commissioned it two years ago at his wife's passing.

The grey jaconet muslin had a modest neckline--slightly bulging--with short puffed sleeves. The material fell gracefully to the ground, ending with four delicate flounces.

The flounces were new. They had to have been added to the hemline because this woman was much taller than his diminutive mother.

Elaina Wattell stopped and then turned to the butler. "Mr. Doyle, I appreciate you, you know, carrying me up to Fannie's bedroom last night. That was very kind. I'm sorry to have been such a bother."

Doyle was a polished butler. Many would say the consummate butler, however at this woman's grateful words, he blushed a crimson shade of pink.

Instead of replying, he cleared his throat, nodded his head, and then exited the Library. Thankfully, he left the door open.

The woman glanced around the room with wide eyes as if she were devouring the contents all in one gulp. For a moment, her attention was captured by the family portrait hanging over the Library's ornate marble fireplace. The painting was of his parents and him, when he was eight.

For some reason he did not want her to focus on anything but him... as he was now.

He stood, greeted her with a bow, and then gestured toward the long couch bench a few feet away from his desk. "Miss Wattell, please, have a seat."

She sat demurely, folded her hands in her lap, and then raised her steady gaze to regard him. "You wanted to see me... sir?"

He could not find fault with her impeccable manners. "Yes. I trust you slept well?"

At her nod, he cleared his throat. "Good. We need to continue our discussion from last night." As he walked back to his desk, he adjusted the precise bow on his cravat. "I will wager both of us were a trifle under the weather."

He was rewarded with a smile. "That's one way of putting it." She gave a shrug. "Frankly I don't think I've ever slept as hard as I did last night. I actually just woke up a half hour ago."

The image of Elaina Wattell resting on his sitting room settee bombarded his thoughts. Her long neck... her flutter of dark lashes... her chestnut brown hair arranged in a chignon with side curls, appeared just as shiny this morning. Her plump lips, her pert nose, her flawless complexion... how had she possibly readied herself so quickly?

Charles noticed his Sèvres teacup cooling on his desk, and that sparked a thought. "Miss Wattell, have you eaten this morning?"

Her eyelashes flickered down. "Well, no. There wasn't time."

Standing, he strode over to the open oak door, signaled to a footman, and ordered a variety of breakfast foods to be brought to the Library. Then he returned to his desk.

"My apologies, Miss Wattell. It was not my intention to deprive you of nourishment."

"One skipped meal won't hurt." She shrugged again. "Listen, I have to be frank. I realize that my being here at Wolfeshire Park is unusual. I also know that my circumstances are... unorthodox. I guess you could say I'm rather needy right now. I have no home, no friends, no money, no clothes, and no prospects."

He steepled his fingertips together. "Go on."

She leaned forward, close to the edge of the bench, closer to him. "What I really need is time. Time to figure out what I'm going to do. So, I guess what I'm asking is would you mind letting me stay here a while? It wouldn't be long. I could work. Fannie could show me what she does as a housemaid. Or maybe I could help in the kitchen."

Of all the favors that could have been asked of him, he never imagined a favor so inconsequential. She could have asked or demanded he set her up in her own household. She could have bargained to become his new mistress. She could have set the Bon Ton on its ears with her remarkable good looks.

Unable to sit any longer, he paced from one end of the Library to the other, and then back again.

She stayed quiet for a minute, and then spoke. "That's a lovely family portrait hanging over the fireplace. That little boy is you, right? Robbie looks just like you."

"Robert," he corrected, but truthfully he no longer felt consumed with anger about the alternative name for his son as he had yesterday.

Doyle then entered with a platter overflowing with tempting breakfast aromas. Setting the platter on the side table where she sat, he removed silver covers on a bowl of oatmeal with cream, grilled eggs, bacon, an assortment of breads with colorful jams, along with cakes, Bath buns, and brioche.

"Tea, *Mademoiselle?* Coffee? Hot chocolate?" the butler asked.

Elaina Wattell nibbled on that plump lower lip of hers. "Oh. Just a cup of coffee for me, thank you, Mr. Doyle." She then looked over at Charles. "This is very kind of you. Can I prepare you a plate?"

Whatever manner of woman she was, she had impeccable behavior.

Once again he silently approved of her actions. He inclined his head. "No, thank you, Miss Wattell. I have already eaten."

After Doyle left, and again, he left the door open, Charles poured himself more tea and sat back down behind his desk. He waited for her to finish. The woman must not have had a hardy appetite because she only ate one egg, one piece of bacon, and one slice of shortbread.

She dotted her lips with the napkin. "The food is absolutely delicious. Thank you. You must have an excellent Cook."

"Mrs. Parsons has been at Wolfeshire Park for almost twenty years."

Elaina glanced around the room again and then focused on him. "So, have you thought about what I said? About working here temporarily?"

Setting a ledger to the side of the desk, Charles then folded his hands in front of him. "Tell me about this hypnosis that you mentioned. Perhaps it is the same as 'Mesmerism', named after Franz Mesmer, a German physician. He recently died, five years ago. I have looked it up."

He waved a hand around the room. "This is a Library, after all.

"You have a very impressive library." She nibbled on her lower lip again.

Again, she pleased him. "In any event, Miss Wattell, Mesmerism pertains to a person being in a state of focused attention, and supposedly has increased suggestibility. There are no mentions of transferring location."

She nodded. "Yes, I know. But Mesmerism does sound like hypnosis. My good friend, Leila, did some studying on her own and thought it might be good for me."

"Why did she think it would be good for you?"

Elaina twisted her hands. "I... I suffered a trauma when I was young. Just two years old. My family and friends were celebrating my birthday in the woods by a lake. I wandered off and got lost. I guess I fell into a ravine or something, and then they found me three days later." She shivered. "I really don't remember, but honestly, I don't like being alone--I mean *really* alone--especially in the woods. My friend thought she could help."

She blinked her eyes, perhaps to drive away tears. "Anyway, enough of that. I apologize that I'm taking up your time with... my problems, but as you can imagine, I'm at a loss here. I'm thinking if I could just have time to think, maybe I can figure out what I should do."

Charles stared down at his hands. Her story moved him. *She* moved him. This was truly all she wanted from him: time to contemplate her strange situation.

Although he did not fully comprehend her peculiar circumstances, he could certainly allow her some time to remain here at the Park. He could be magnanimous. Her staying here would not make one iota of difference one way or another. Except that...

Except that she was a very desirable female.

"Miss Wattell, I--"

"Noooo!" A bellowing cry followed by stomping feet rushed into the Library. It was Robert: wild-eyed, red faced, and bushy haired.

His son halted in the middle of the room in between the desk and Elaina on the bench, his miniature fists set on his puny hips.

He glared at Charles. "She's mine! I found her! You can't take her from me!"

Astonishment did not even cover what Charles was feeling. This kind of rebellious behavior had never happened before. Elaina was obviously astonished as well. She set her coffee back on the platter.

Charles said as calmly as he could, "Robert, what the devil--"

"No!" Robert dashed over to the desk and reached into the jar containing writing accessories. He pulled out a pair of sharp scissors.

"You can't, you won't have her. She's mine, I tell you!" After those words, Robert stretched his small arm out toward Charles' head and snipped.

As if time stood still, Charles watched as a long, thick lock of his hair fell slowly down onto his desk.

"Robbie, no!" Elaina shouted.

Charles blindly felt the side of his head. The rough feel of uneven hair greeted him. The missing piece lay on the desk. He picked up the shorn lock and stared at it.

May the good Lord help him but he wanted nothing more than to whip his son.

# Chapter Five

*Omigosh!* The Library went from regimented order to out-of-control chaos in two seconds flat. Not only did the Duke shoot icy daggers from his dark eyes at his now howling son, but Mr. Doyle burst into the room, wringing his hands and looking like he'd rather be anyplace else.

The elderly figure of Robbie's nanny, Price, also rushed in. The woman stopped, mid-step, to shake and moan and mop at her weepy eyes with a large cotton handkerchief. She was absolutely hysterical.

And when the housekeeper, Mrs. Riddles and Trundles, the lady's maid, joined the fray, Elaina worried things would only get worse. It was like a three-ring circus.

Price blubbered, "Oh my eyes! I'm undone fer sure! Master Robert'll be me very death!"

Elaina had to take charge. She hurried over to the group. "Mrs. Riddles, Miss Trundles, would you please help Mrs. Price outside? Take her someplace quiet where she can calm her nerves. Maybe a nice cup of hot tea might help."

"Yes, *Mademoiselle*. Of course." Mrs. Riddles bobbed her head, sending her chins to wagging. She took the elderly woman by the arm. "And, just so you know, 'tis a spinster, Price is. She's never been married."

Elaina almost snorted. As if marriage status had anything to do with this crazy mess!

Trundle situated herself by Price's other side. She blinked her tired eyes at Elaina. "Yes, *Mademoiselle*. We'll do just that. How... very inappropriate this all is."

After the women left, Elaina turned to Mr. Doyle. She had to raise her voice because Robbie's young lungs filled the Library with his distress.

"Mr. Doyle, I can fix this. If you would, can you bring me two sheets, like small bedsheets, and some combs and a brush? Oh, and also, if you have a mirror--you know, a looking-glass? Handheld, if possible."

The butler darted his gaze to his employer who remained mute, then nodded and went on his way.

All of this took a minute or two. Nibbling on her lower lip, she inhaled deeply and gathered her courage. She approached Mr. Mount Vesuvius as he got ready to blow.

She stood in front of him. "Sir, I can fix your hair. I'll just use these scissors to even things out, and you'll be as good as new."

The man's eyes narrowed. "As good as new. A comforting sentiment, Miss Wattell." He fingered his uneven hair. "My valet is my personal barber; tell me why I should trust you."

She picked up the scissors and open and closed them. They were sharp and lightweight. She could work with them.

"I think I told you, I'm a hairstylist by trade. A coiffeuse."

He eyed the scissors with suspicion. "Can you silence that caterwauling boy?"

Instead of answering him, she winked, and then sat next to Robbie on the leather bench across from the desk. She held out her arms so the boy could take refuge, if he wanted.

He wanted. He hurled himself into her, making a small "oof" noise upon impact. Thankfully, his crying grew less and less until it stopped.

"Robbie," she spoke into his hair. "That was very naughty of you. You can't disrespect your father like that. And your nanny, why, the poor woman is beside herself."

"I know," the boy sniffed into the gathered bodice on her gown. "I sorry. But you're mine, Elle. You belong to me. I found you. I won't let him take you from me. I won't let him send you away."

This poor boy was so very lonely. Her heart actually shuddered with his unhappiness.

She glanced at the Duke. He continued to sit behind his desk, glaring at his son. She shivered at the man's unforgiving expression.

"Robbie," she softly whispered. "You have to apologize for your terrible actions. To your father, and to your nanny. You've hurt them deeply and you have to take responsibility for your actions. You're seven years old now, and that means you're a big boy."

Pulling away from her, he looked at her with sorrowful eyes. "Will you stay here, Elle? Stay with me?"

"Robbie, I can't promise that. You know I don't belong here."

"But you do," he sing-songed. "I found you."

Elaina huffed a sigh. "Well, tell you what. Your father and I will have a little talk, okay? But first, you have to apologize to him and promise to be a good boy. I know you can be a very good boy when you want to be."

Robbie turned to look at his father. His lower lip stuck out. "He hates me."

She tried to hide her smile. "No, your father doesn't hate you. He loves you very much. He's just, um, disappointed in your actions."

Robbie skewed his lips to the side, then took a deep breath. He shivered for a moment, and then stilled.

She patted him on the back to urge him forward. "Now, why don't you apologize and I'll see if I can fix his hair. Then I'm sure he'll feel better."

This whole time, the Duke watched but didn't say a word. She had no idea what he was thinking, but surely he would receive his son's apology.

Fingers crossed. Dukes were, most likely, a little high in the instep.

Robbie trudged his way over to the desk, stood in front of it, and then straightened his shoulders. With his gaze down, he murmured, "I... I am sorry for what I did, sir."

The Duke's face was impassive. Honestly, his face could've been carved in stone.

Mr. Doyle noiselessly entered the Library, nodded at the Duke, and then handed Elaina a basket filled with hair accessories.

The Duke's stern eyebrows came to a vee at the bridge of his nose. "Robert, you and I shall have a talk later this afternoon. For now, go with Mr. Doyle. I am certain he has chores for you."

The boy raised his brilliant blue gaze to look at his father. "What about Elle?"

"As you know, Miss Wattell has kindly offered to fix my hair. Now go."

Robbie took a step in her direction. "Can you cut my hair too, Elle?"

Ooh. He was such a sweet little boy. Or rather, he could be such a sweet little boy if he wanted to be.

Standing, she walked over to the desk. "If you like. Later, okay?"

He grinned, showing off his missing tooth. "Okay!"

The boy then joined Mr. Doyle and walked out of the Library.

"Close the door, Doyle, and see that we are not disturbed."

"Yes, sir," was the butler's reply. He then closed the door.

And now she was alone with Mr. Mount Vesuvius, and that meant she was a little bit nervous.

"So." She handed him the handheld mirror. "First I think you should see the damage. Then you need to decide if you trust me to work with your hair."

He took the mirror and examined the shorn edges. "I suppose it could have been worse. You are certain about this? I look like I have had a run in with a pair of scissors, which, of course, I have."

"I'm definitely sure. I cut men's hair all the time. Or, at least I did, when I was home." She folded her arms across her chest. "So, are we good? Are you going to be comfortable with me... doing the cutting?"

A slight smile lifted his lips. "I cannot say if I will be comfortable, but I will tolerate it, Miss Wattell."

"Good. You won't be sorry."

After taking another look at him in his too-fine-to-be-wearing-in-the-morning clothes, she suggested, "You know, you really should take off your tailcoat and that thing, that complicated cravat around your neck. You should just be in your shirt and waistcoat."

He lifted an eyebrow. "That sounds rather scandalous, Miss Wattell. Or as Trundle likes to say, inappropriate."

A joke! He was making a joke.

She felt heat rise on her cheeks. "Well, it will make it easier for me to cut your hair. But if you feel, um, inappropriately dressed, I guess I'll have to manage."

Standing, he removed both articles of clothing. "I would not want to put you to the blush, Miss Wattell." He paused. "However, I see I am too late."

She pressed her lips together. "Cute."

After he sat back down, she knelt on the carpeted floor and arranged one of the bed sheets around his desk chair to catch the shorn locks that would soon tumble down.

From her position, she looked up at him. "By the way, I don't know your name. You're a duke--that I know--but what do I call you?"

He held out his hand to help her to her feet. "The Duke of Wolfeshire. The eighth Duke of Wolfeshire, actually. But my name is Charles. Charles Robert Burnley."

Inclining his head, he pronounced, "You may call me 'sir' or 'Your Grace.'"

Whoa. She had to bite back her laughter. "Really? Cool. Okay, *Your Grace,*" she couldn't help snickering. "It's time to get started."

She used the other bedsheet as a hairdressing cape and arranged it around his broad shoulders and tucking it into the neckline of his white shirt. "First, I like to give a brief massage of the neck and shoulders to help you relax and make you more comfortable. Are you okay with that?"

It took him a while to answer, but then he nodded.

She dug her fingers into his shoulders and began the massage. "Ooh, you're tight."

"Hmmn," was his reply.

Actually, it was a pleasure kneading and rubbing his skin. So much so that she gave a longer massage than she usually did. When she started on his scalp, he jumped.

"What the devil is that for?"

"Just to relax you, *Your Grace.* You *are* very tense."

"Hmmn," was his reply again.

She continued with the massage using her knowledge of phrenology--the study of the shapes and protuberances on the head. An area in the back of the skull was supposed to deal with parental love so naturally she focused on that--for Robbie's sake. Then she removed a brush and comb set from the basket and began to play with the Duke's hair, to see which way the curls formed.

"Your hair is very fine and silky. It's a pleasure to work with."

He had no comment, and she had to grin.

Although she was a slow starter, soon she began to snip, snip away. "I typically use clippers on men's hair, but..."

But what could she say? Electric clippers hadn't been invented yet.

"But?" he inquired.

She had to improvise. "But these steel shears are perfectly sharp for the job."

Every now and then she had to tip his head slightly to get the correct angle. At first he resisted her, but then got used to her touch.

Part of a stylist's job was to cajole clients with conversation to pass the time and keep them entertained. Not with this fellow, though. After all, what does one say to amuse a duke?

It didn't take long to even out his hair. The rhythm of her scissors trimming his hair was almost... mesmerizing.

She grinned again. The style was shorter than what he evidently was used to wearing, but he looked good. Then again, no matter what, he would've looked exceptional.

Stepping to the front of him, she lifted strands of his hair on either side to make sure the lengths matched. Pleased with her creation, she stepped back from him and admired her handiwork.

"*Voilá!* You look magnificent! See for yourself." Removing the hairdressing cape, she then handed him the mirror.

Now that she had finished, the sensations of being so close to him, the scent of him, touching him, running her fingers through his hair just about overwhelmed her. Before, she'd been able to keep those sensations at bay since she'd been occupied, but now... woof!

She backed away even further. "So, what do you think? What's the verdict?"

Honestly, that man had a poker face that just wouldn't quit. She had no idea what was rattling around in his brain. Did he smile? No. Did he seem pleased? No.

She had to be truthful; his dark mop of hair had been transformed into a thing of beauty.

Folding her arms across her chest, she waited for... His Grace.

He set the mirror down. "This has been an interesting experience for me."

Well, la-di-da!

She skewed her lips like she'd seen his son do. "And your hair?"

"It is tolerable."

Ooh! She puffed up with outrage. Her eyes must've been flashing lightning storms.

"Tolerable? Listen, you... you..."

He stood there with a slight smile on his face and a twinkle lighting his dark eyes.

He was amused?

Taking a deep breath, she calmed herself... and kept her lips shut.

Slipping back into his tailcoat, he lifted one of his infernal eyebrows. "I look magnificent?"

To use his word: hmmn. She focused on cleaning up. "Well, maybe. I don't know. Then, again, what do I know? I'm only a peasant to you... *Your Grace.*"

He grabbed her wrist. "You are not a peasant."

His skin was so hot on hers. So hot that she actually gasped.

They stood for a moment not moving, staring into each other's eyes.

Then she pulled away again.

"Tell me, Miss Wattell, how are you so good with my son? How did he get attached to you in such a short time?"

She continued her clean up. "I don't really know. I'm guessing that he's lonely. He's probably missing his mother and his grandmother."

When she moved to get down on the floor to pick up the bedsheet with all the cut hair, he touched her again, this time his hand circling her upper arm.

Again, his touch burned into her skin. "Leave this. Mr. Doyle will handle it."

She glanced down at his hand, still curled around her upper arm. She lifted her own eyebrow.

He released her. "I did not give you my answer, Miss Wattell. About staying at Wolfeshire Park."

Ooh! All her systems went on red alert! Wanting to jump out of her skin, she took a breath and looked at him. All she saw was a pulse beating by the corner of his eye.

"And?" she prompted.

He inclined his head. "It is my greatest pleasure to invite you to stay with us, here at the Park. For however long as you wish."

"That's great! Thanks!" Thank goodness! Now she didn't have to worry about getting thrown out on the street, as it were. "I'll tell Fannie and she can show me--"

"There will be no work required, Miss Wattell. You will be my guest."

She shook her head so hard, her side ringlets almost flew out from her face. "No. I mean, I thank you but I've got to earn my keep. I assure you I can do other kinds of work, in addition to cutting hair."

He ran his finger up and down his long sideburn. "Perhaps there is something."

Her heart lurched. What was he going to say? "Yes?"

"If you would, you could be my son's governess. Temporary, of course, for as long as you are here. I am certain you are capable of the job. In such a short time, you have made my son extremely happy. Something, I fear, the dear boy has not felt in quite some time."

Wow. That was a great idea, and definitely not too arduous. Also, it would provide consistency to Robbie's life.

"That sounds really good. I'll just need to have a curriculum so Robbie--"

The Duke lifted both eyebrows.

"Um, Robert," she corrected. "So Robert is on track for learning what he needs."

"Mr. Doyle will be a help in that area. There is one other matter. The governess' quarters are next to my son's. That is where you will be staying."

"Oh." Her eyes widened. "I mean, well, I told you I don't like to be alone. I'd rather stay with Fannie, if she doesn't mind."

The Duke reached out and took her hand. This time he held it gently. "There is an adjoining door between the rooms. If you wish, you could leave that door open. In that way, you would not be alone."

She trembled. She could feel it... and if she could feel it then he could, too.

"Well, okay. Maybe that will work out. I hope so. Thank you." She removed her hand from his. "I'll go now... and talk with Mr. Doyle."

Brushing his hand through his newly cut hair, the Duke nodded at her. "My thanks for fixing my hair, Miss Wattell. I find I do like this shorter look. Very much so."

"Oh. Sure. You're welcome." With those words she opened the Library door and then scuttled out into the corridor.

Holy cow! That man made her blood pressure skyrocket! And her heart pound. And every darn internal part of her tingle.

*Down, girl. Down.*

Back home where she belonged, she wished for a duke. Did this mean, in some impossible way, that she wished for *him?*

**\* \* \* \***

Shooting was an agreeable way to spend a few hours. The camaraderie between four aristocrats plus one plump-in-the-pocket mister was always enjoyable. If any one of the Pack was not in the best of spirits, then this particular sport was guaranteed to smooth the gentleman's ruffled feathers.

Today's particular walking shoot for the Park's plentiful red grouse had been successful in not only yielding birds for the tenants' kitchens, but also in dispensing any "foul" dispositions.

Jules Greensby had set aside his indolence to eagerly plow over the rolling hills and grassy terrain found in the northern regions of the Wolfeshire estate. The resulting physical activity had given a decided rosy glow to the man's chubby cheeks.

As a contrast, Lord Kenneth Martiz had opted to walk the grounds instead of indulging in shooting. He had complained the noise and smoke from the rifles rattled his injured head.

Charles had to admit the shooting had given him a slight megrim as well. To be truthful, that *and* his son's unusual rebellion in the Library added to the megrim.

Then again, the overly sensuous experience of Elaina Wattell massaging his shoulders and head was bound to keep him awake this night. May the dear Lord help him, at the time it was all he could do to remain seated and not savagely sweep her in his arms and take her on the floor.

Madness!

He wiped the perspiration that had formed from underneath his shooting cap. True, it was a hot August day, but that was not the reason for the sweat.

Taking a rest on a grouping of rocks while Greensby and Lord Otto Blankton continued with the shoot, Charles patted one of his hunting dogs. He could not seem to think of anything, of anyone but Elaina Wattell, with her magic hands and the sensual sway of her sweet form.

"You look as if you have something serious on your mind, Wolfe." Lord Nome walked over, sat next to him, and then set his rifle down by his side. "On the way through the house, I noticed your son polishing the silver in the butler's pantry. Is there a shortage of help at the Park? Have you suffered a reversal of fortunes?"

Nome was a downy fellow. He would not stop his questions until he learned the truth.

"Chores for the boy, Nome. He has run unrestrained for far too long. Requires discipline."

Charles had to change the subject. "Where did Martiz get to?"

"The Viscount decided to sit it out two hills ago. As far as I know he's with a few of your men, looking over the booty of grouse carcasses. Probably spouting some colorful phrases as well." Nome pulled off his hunting cap to brush back his unruly hair. "Refresh my memory, Wolfe. What are the plans for tonight?"

Tonight. Tonight that intriguing young woman would be sleeping next to Robert's room... with the door ajar. Charles had to withhold his smile.

Instead, he glanced up at the beautiful visage of undulating hills and wind-tossed clouds. In the distance, a flurry of agitated birds took to the skies only to be scattered when one of the Pack fired his rifle.

"Tonight? Yes, it will be rather informal, Nome. I thought we could enjoy another round of whist. You know, rest our old bones up for tomorrow's foxhunt."

Nome patted one of the hunting dogs on its mottled white head. Then he sighed. "So, Wolfe, I don't mean to complain about your hospitality however, I've had my fill of listening to Blankton bemoaning his sad tale of having his pockets to let. That's all he did last night after you deserted us. The curst thing about it all was that the beggar won. He has more feathers to fly with than ever before."

"Good for Blankton."

"A pox on Blankton," Nome growled. "And another thing, Wolfe, I find I am missing the fairer sex. All these men and no women is not natural."

Charles slapped at his friend's knee. "Saturday night we shall have an informal gathering. Two of my neighbors have well-favored daughters. Some country dancing, a game or two... that will lift your spirits."

Nome shrugged his rather broad shoulders. Then he gestured toward Charles' hair. "Been meaning to ask you, you went to bed with a raggedy head and this afternoon you have the latest style *à la Titus*. It is brilliant! Who does your hair, man? Your valet? Lend him to me. I want these locks of mine to be shorn, too."

By all that was holy, there was no way on God's good Earth that Charles would allow Elaina Wattell to touch, to massage, to even be near that rakehell's head. No. He did not even want her in Nome's general vicinity.

She was his, and that was that.

Then Charles nodded. Now he understood his son's fixation for her.

"Sorry, Nome. My valet has to leave on an urgent errand. Off to London, no less. Perhaps when Wilkins has completed his task."

"Unfortunate." Nome yawned.

The first thing Charles would do when he returned to his home was to send Wilkins to London on the pretense of ordering a new morning coat by London master George Stultz, but in reality, ordering a wardrobe for Miss Elaina Wattell.

By residing at his house, she was under Charles' protection. He felt responsible for her; he felt an unsuitable attraction.

**\* \* \* \***

After talking with Mr. Doyle about the duties of a governess, Elaina then asked if it was all right if she first used the kitchen to make a particular recipe, and then go to the Duke's Library to gather the information she needed to prepare lesson plans.

"As for the kitchen, I am certain Mrs. Parsons will be agreeable. What is the recipe for?" the great man inquired.

Elaina felt a burn of heat on her cheeks. "Actually, it's a very mild shampoo, made with water, chamomile flowers, and some soap flakes."

She'd used this recipe on one of her twenty-first century clients who'd been extremely allergic to commercial hair products. The shampoo didn't take long to prepare and it worked like a charm.

Elaina needed this organic hair wash now. Why? Because the soap and the shampoo here were too harsh. She'd found out these items were made with lye and ash from the fireplace. At least the products used in the servants' quarters did. Lye had been known to leave a burn on the skin, and that was something she wanted to avoid.

"I am assured Mrs. Parsons will agree, *Mademoiselle* Elaina. As for the Library," the butler intoned as he inclined his head. "Everything you require for Master Robert's academic learning can be found His Grace's vast collection of books."

The Library was impressive, true, but she had to wonder if any of the books had information that could be used to teach a young child.

"And, may I say, *Mademoiselle*, every servant here at Wolfeshire Park is delighted you will be instructing the young master. He is quite taken with you."

Robbie *was* taken with her. Fixated, even. But maybe it was a good thing, for him and for her.

"He's a darling boy," she agreed. "Well, I'll let you get back to your work, Mr. Doyle. I need to get busy so I have something to teach tomorrow."

Leaving the butler in his pantry, she quickly made her way to the kitchen. As she had said to Mr. Doyle, formulating the shampoo was easy, and soon she had a few bottles of the fragrant shampoo.

Next up was the Library. She hurried through the servants' quarters and into the main section of the grand house. It didn't take her long to find the Duke's extraordinary Library.

Entering this somber room, she stood for a moment, glancing around the bookshelves. The book spines were by and large uniform in size; the colors were mostly amber, green, and dark blue. For a moment, she felt a bit dizzy just looking at the stacks of these volumes.

She shook her head to collect herself. The room was completely empty of life except for a potted cactus plant sitting on the front edge of his large double pedestal desk--very pretty, and also prickly. Look but don't touch. Actually, she was reminded of its owner.

Smiling at that thought, she then shook off the feeling that she was intruding on the Duke's privacy. That didn't stop her, though. She walked over to his desk. Making herself at home on his comfortable chair, she paused to remember what had happened a few hours ago right here in this very place. Robbie's bad behavior, the Duke's outrage at his hair's mutilation, the feel of the scissors' cold steel in her hands...

How very close she'd stood to him, so intimately close in his personal space. Running her fingers through his fine, silky hair. Inhaling his manly scent. And then the sheer magic... or was that shear?... of creating a spectacular coiffure specifically for him.

Absolutely fabulous!

She allowed herself one more minute to indulge in these memories, then got back to business. She removed a sheet of fine, vellum stationery set in a box on the desk. First, she'd write out the list of well-rounded courses required for a seven-year-old boy--at least according to Mr. Doyle. Time to get started.

Teaching English, including reading and writing: that would probably be the easiest.

Teaching French and Latin: nope. She'd have to take a pass on those subjects.

Teaching science: well, as long as that particular science existed in 1820, she'd be okay. No quantum physics on the agenda!

Teaching mathematics: math really didn't change much, so she could work with that.

Teaching geography: as long as she could find a current map of the world, she could fudge this subject.

Teaching the arts, like drawing and music: hmmn. Okay, she could probably take a stab at the arts. Sketching the landscape and discussing the fabulous paintings on Wolfeshire Park's walls, sure, that would work.

For music, well, she could teach Robbie songs. They could do a sing-along. She could even play the piano by ear. Maybe even read the notes on sheets of music. She'd done that growing up; maybe she could do it again.

As for physical activity, they could play ball, or catch, or other activities that involved running. Maybe even a bit of swimming if there was a lake nearby... if that wouldn't be too scandalous... or *inappropriate!*

How much time ticked by she had no idea. After scouring the library walls, she'd pulled out a few books to help her devise her schedule for each day. Surprisingly, she liked doing this. Maybe she was cut out to be a teacher rather than a hairstylist.

Ha ha. No!

She was busy scrutinizing an atlas she found, evidently made by a celebrated map-maker by the name of Thomas Moule when she heard the sound of footsteps entering the Library. Very light footsteps, like a child's.

Looking up, she saw Robbie's grinning and missing-one-tooth smile.

"Elle!" he shouted as he ran to the desk and then into her outstretched arms. "Good-O! I've been looking everywhere for you."

Her heart nearly burst. It was so good to be wanted. How could she have known that she was missing this type of connection?

"Hi, Robbie. It's good to see you. What have you been up to on this fine August day?"

"Chores," he said with disgust, pouting his perfect lips. He pulled a needlepoint-cushioned armchair over to the side of the desk and then plopped down on it. "I've polished silver, scraped melted wax from candleholders, counted too many plates, and ho, can you believe? I dusted the furniture!"

Since his feet didn't reach the floor, he kicked them in the air and against the chair's wooden legs.

Elaina withheld her smile. "Well, I can guess you were a big help to Mr. Doyle."

"Maybe." Robbie shot her a mischievous smile. "He said I'm a good worker. I did a fine job."

"Great! That's what we want to hear." She couldn't help wondering if his father had that "talk" with him about his behavior.

As if Robbie knew what she was thinking, the boy drooped his head. "I know. Elle, I know I was bad to cut my father's hair."

She nodded. "Yep, that *was* pretty awful."

He then lifted his head so she could see his sparkling eyes. "Mr. Doyle told me you're staying! You're going t'be my new governess."

He jumped out of the chair and gave her a tight hug. "I'm happy."

*Mmm!* She lost herself in his hug. He smelled like lemon polish and beeswax and little boy sweat.

Kissing the top of his head, she then sat back in the chair. "I'm happy, too. But you do know me being here is only temporary. I don't belong and I have to somehow get back to my own home."

"I want you to stay," he mumbled as he found his way onto her lap for a very comforting cuddle. "I found you, Elle. You're supposed to stay with me."

She sighed. He spoke with the certainly that only the very young could have.

How odd to be indulging in a cuddle in this very business-like room! Enjoying the closeness with Robbie, she suddenly had an idea. She could use another perspective on her own particular problem, no matter how outlandish the answer might be.

"So, Robbie, maybe you can help me figure out a way to solve my problem. Would you like to try?"

"Maybe." He looked up at her with his gorgeous blue-eyed gaze. "What do I have to do?"

"Easy. Just think about what I tell you. This is like a puzzle and it has to be figured out. Here goes: what would you do if you were talking with a friend. Your friend wanted to help you get over a fear-- something you'd been afraid of for a very long time. Suddenly, while she--"

"He," Robbie insisted.

"Okay, while *he* was talking, you got very tired so you closed your eyes. In the air was a peculiar scent--an herbal scent, and it seemed to lull you asleep. Then you woke up and you were very far away, so far away that the year wasn't even the same. As far away as, maybe, from here to... Paris or maybe even the Americas."

"Or the antipodes!" Robbie interjected. "My father talks about that a lot. Do y'know, New Zealand is the antipode from London."

Smart boy! "Okay, the antipodes. Now, since you're in such a strange place, how would you get home? Remember, the year is different, too."

"Hmmn." Robbie settled into her, leaning his cheek against the jugular notch at the base of her neck. He spoke against her skin. "What are you frightened of, Elle? I know my fear: losing you!"

Oh good gosh. He was such a sweet little boy. She hugged him even closer.

Closing her eyes tightly to drive away any unexpected tears, she continued, "Well, you don't have to be scared of that. I think I'll probably be here for a while."

Taking a deep breath, she confided, "So, my fear is being alone, especially in a forest."

"But that's where I found you--you were alone in a forest! So that means you don't have to be afraid anymore, Elle. I will always find you!"

She thought about his words. Somehow the thought of being alone in a strange place, even being outside, didn't seem as frightening as before.

It felt as if a huge load was suddenly lifted off her shoulders. She couldn't help smiling! "You're right, Robbie. I didn't have time to be scared when I woke up because you were already by my side."

As far as Robbie was concerned: problem solved! He squiggled off her lap and stood with his small fists akimbo on his hips.

He faced her head on. "Tell me about that smell, that herb."

Good point. "It's called thyme and it was growing around the tree where I sat. Thyme smells like... lemon, and grass, and maybe a bit of lavender."

"Time?" Robbie reached across the desk and pulled a sheet of paper from the box. Then he grabbed a pencil. "Like a different time because it's a different year?"

"Well, actually the herb is spelt t-h-y-m-e. Odd spelling, I know."

He sat himself down on the carpet and placed the paper on the exposed wooden floorboards surrounding the room. Then he got busy putting pencil to paper.

"But, Elle, herbs sound like something a country healer uses. Herbs and potions are like magic. We have a healer here; she lives near the closest village. She's old but maybe she can help you. Maybe she can cure you of that fear."

Elaina had to think about that. Hmmn, after all, why not consult with this healer? She didn't have anything to lose. Maybe this woman could induce hypnosis and wave a cutting of fresh thyme in the air. Maybe when Elaina then focused on what she wanted, she'd concentrate on going home. Maybe that could actually happen.

With both them now occupied, she with thoughts of returning to her own century, and he with... she glanced at his penciled drawing... with a vivid sketch of some type of lizard monster, the time passed companionably.

Soon heavy footsteps sounded in the hallway, approaching the Library. Mr. Doyle entered and bowed. *"Mademoiselle* Elaina, Master Robert."

"Mr. Doyle, how's everything? Rob... Robert and I are getting ready for our lessons tomorrow."

His stern gaze flicker over them, and if she wasn't mistaken, she thought she saw a hint of a smile.

"Indeed. Master Robert, your father wishes to talk with you in the Gold Drawing Room."

Robbie's lower lip protruded, but he got off the floor and then handed his drawing to her. "This is for you, Elle."

She took the paper. The figure on it was very fierce, indeed! "Is this supposed to be anyone I know?"

Robbie just grinned. "Elle, I see you at dinner in the nursery?"

"I'm looking forward to it. I'll see you soon. Thank you for the picture."

Robbie nodded and then he and the butler walked out of the Library.

Elaina watched them leave. Now would come the "talk." What would the Duke say? Would he scold his son? Would he... beat him?

Shivering although it wasn't chilly in the room, she turned back to her lesson notes all the while keeping her fingers crossed for Robbie's sake.

# Chapter Six

Finally, this long day was over. Elaina could barely stay on her feet as she walked through the adjoining door from Robbie's bedroom and into the assigned bedroom for the governess.

He was an easy child to put to bed, not that she'd had experience in that area. She had no brother or sister; nor did her mother have any siblings. Her father's family lived on the Pacific coast so she hadn't grown up with cousins.

But Robbie was uncomplicated. As she'd done last night, she read him one of his books, then told him a fairytale: "Jack And The Giant Beanstalk", and lastly, sang him the same tune as yesterday.

He liked routine. As soon as she was on the last refrain, his eyes closed. He was out.

His "talk" with his father must not have been difficult because when she saw him at dinnertime, his blue eyes had been clear, untroubled. His cheeks rosy, his laugh carefree, he'd been a perfect little companion.

She could admit to herself: she was growing very fond of him.

But now she had herself to take care of.

The governess' bedroom was very bright, not at all like the rather dreary room Fannie had to sleep in. All four walls were covered with *fleur-de-lis* patterned wallpaper and a wall-to-wall checked carpet covered the floor.

The room boasted of a single-sized bed, a chest of drawers, a large wardrobe, a nightstand, a small table with two chairs, plus two decent-sized windows to light up the bedroom in the daytime.

The feature she liked the most was a side area off to the right of the door. This was her "bathroom," containing a hip bath filled with water, a transportable commode, a dressing table holding a pitcher of water and a bowl to wash her face, and a rather speckled wall mirror.

True luxury, indeed!

She'd worry about how she should dump the bathwater out later. Right now, she closed the privacy doors and soaked herself in this tiny bronze tub while the water was still lukewarm.

*Mmm.*

After toweling off, she slipped on an ankle-length nightgown, also highwaisted, with roomy bell sleeves and a row of lace decorating the hem. Although this nightgown had plenty of material to cover her, it seemed to be made of very fine cotton. So fine that it was a bit translucent.

Elaina couldn't help laughing. How *inappropriate!*

Just as she was combing her wet hair, a knock sounded at the door. As far as she knew, she didn't have a bathrobe so she grabbed a wet towel and held it up to cover her front.

She opened the door.

On the other side stood Trundles in a dark green scoop-neck gown, mob cap, and waist-to-floor apron. The woman's tired eyes seemed to plead with Elaina.

*"Mademoiselle* Elaina, *Mademoiselle* Elaina, why did not you let me know you wanted to prepare for bed? This is most inappropriate. Most inappropriate."

Elaina stood aside to let the woman come in. "I don't understand. I didn't know I needed to... to ask permission?"

Trundle had the audacity to remove the wet towel and then helped Elaina into the chair in front of the mirror. "I shall dry your hair, *Mademoiselle* Elaina. Please, I am a lady's maid. Allow me to take care of you."

Well, having her hair brushed by someone else certainly wasn't a hardship!

As Trundles combed, she used another towel to blot the wetness from Elaina's long hair.

The woman's lips grew pinched. "If you please, *Mademoiselle* Elaina, my mistress is gone. One month now. I... I fear, I fear very much the Duke will let me go if there is no need for me at Wolfeshire Park."

She blinked her eyes as if to drive away tears. "And if that happens, whatever will become of me? Where will I go?" She sniffed. "I promise I shall do my very best for you, *Mademoiselle* Elaina."

Good gosh! This poor woman was terrified she'd lose her job.

Elaina shivered a little in the unheated room. After all she'd just been wet and her nightgown was as flimsy as flimsy could be.

"I don't understand how these things work, but I don't think the position of governess has a lady's maid assigned to her, does it?"

The woman reached under the dressing table and removed a quilted blanket. She eagerly placed it around Elaina's shoulders.

"There are no hard and fast rules pertaining to that, *Mademoiselle* Elaina. Indeed, once I heard you are now Master Robert's governess, I petitioned Mr. Doyle and Mrs. Riddles about it. They both agreed it is fitting that you, as governess, have a lady's maid." Trundle bobbed a curtsy.

"Oh." Well, if both the butler and the housekeeper thought this was a good idea, then sure, why not? Having this little schoolmarm of a lady's maid around would make life easier. Plus, Trundle wouldn't have to worry about losing her job, as long as Elaina was living here, anyway.

She smiled up at the woman. "This sounds perfect, then. Thanks. I can use your help, that's for sure! But please, you must call me Elaina, and I'll call you by your first name. What is it?"

The woman tugged on her earlobe. "I am not sure that is appropriate, *Mademoiselle* Elaina."

Elaina heaved a sigh. "Indulge me."

"I am Trudy Trundle, *Mademoiselle* Elaina. If you wish, you can call me Trudy. However, I am certain that I cannot call you by your first name." Her voice wavered. "Please. I would not want Mr. Doyle to be vexed with me."

Elaina smiled and then hugged the quilt around her. "Okay, then. No vexing. So, first thing I'm going to need is a robe. A warm one would be really nice."

Trudy made a pleased little smile. "Of course, *Mademoiselle* Elaina. I shall procure whatever you need. Allow me to take stock of your bedchamber and then I shall return with whatever you require."

Elaina thanked her new lady's maid. Never in a million years would she have thought that she'd be in the pampered position of having her own personal maid. Trudy would certainly be helpful. Any question Elaina had about nineteenth century life, she could ask Trudy.

Maybe Trudy knew the name of the village healer, too. And she'd know the correct way to dispose of dirty bathwater.

While Trudy was busy rummaging through the wardrobe and the chest of drawers, Elaina brushed her nearly dried hair and wound it into a bun atop her head. She glanced longingly at her comfortable looking bed. Soon she'd be under the covers. She couldn't wait to sink into sleep.

**\* \* \* \***

"Ho hum. I *am* waiting for the fun to begin." Alastair Dover, Lord Nome, threw his whist cards down on the table and then got up to pace the border around the Gold Drawing Room. "I'm all dished up for tonight."

He poured another glass of whisky, then gulped down half of the liquid. "Wolfe, I'm in dire need of female company. Who do you have me paired with tomorrow night? Is she a willing sort of female?"

Charles also removed from the table, leaving Lord Otto Blankton and Jules Greensby to continue on by themselves. Lord Martiz was already abed. His war injury was paining him.

Refilling his whisky next to Nome, Charles lowered his voice. "That is hardly a question a gentleman asks, Nome. My neighbors to the north, the MacLevys, have three eligible daughters, and to the west of the Park, the Sinclairs have produced two."

"Five lovelies to dally with. Excellent." Rubbing his hands together, the man persisted with his unsuitable train of thought.

Charles folded his arms across his chest. "There will be no... inappropriate behaviors tomorrow night."

Hell and damn, he sounded like his late mother's lady's maid. He must have been rusticating for too long.

Nome disregarded him. "What about servants? Any worth... you know?"

"Cease and desist, Nome. Upon my honor this will be the last invite to Wolfeshire Park that you receive. Indeed, perhaps you should leave at dawn's break."

Charles left that threat open. No one, *no one* took advantage of his servants.

Nome's response was a shrug. "Just a bit... anxious, if you know what I mean, Wolfe. No harm in it."

Charles turned away from his former friend. Once again he wished that Monday would arrive post haste. The Pack's seven sins of excess no longer appealed to him.

The whist game now broke up with Lord Otto Blankton being the winner again.

"Devil take it, I feel my fortunes are on the mend." Blankton crowed. "Wolfe, may I stay at the Park another week?"

"I think not, Blankton." Charles had to withhold his shudder. He decided to also pace, not that he was feeling anxious, but instead, he was restless. "Monday is the day for all of you to leave."

Greensby settled himself in a comfortable chair near the unlit fireplace. He lifted this morning's issue of *The London Times*. "I daresay we should all go back to London. Such a spectacle there. You will never guess who showed up at Parliament yesterday. Our long absent Queen! The report here says many of the peers cheered her on."

"Cheered her on with a great deal of bawdy talk bandied about, I will wager," Nome muttered.

Greensby, still reading the paper, barked out laughter. "Remember this, gents. If you ever find yourself in a sticky situation, all you have to say is '*Non mi ricordo.*' The Queen's Italian manservant says that: 'I don't recall' over and over again."

The sordid situation back in London with the King and the Queen fueled Charles' fevered thoughts. What a time of civil unrest and monumental crisis.

Doyle broke the stalemate by knocking on the Gold Drawing Room door and then entering. The man's intense gaze darted about and then spotted Charles.

"Your Grace, a missive has just arrived for you." The butler held out a porcelain plate containing a folded letter sealed with wax.

"Thank you, Doyle." Charles picked up the missive. "Wait here a moment."

He then broke the seal and read the brief note.

Blast. One of the young Misses Sinclairs was feeling unwell and would not be able to attend the party at Wolfeshire Park on the morrow.

Not that the absence would be any great concern, however, the dinner numbers would be uneven.

Unless...

He waved Doyle on and then he turned to his tedious guests. "A small matter concerning tomorrow's festivities has just come to my attention. After I attend to this detail, I shall retire for the evening. And so, I bid you all a good night and wish you good fortune at the foxhunt tomorrow."

Charles bowed and then hurried to the staircase. If he remembered correctly, and he was certain that his memory was intact, Elaina Wattell now resided in the governess' bedchamber next to his son's. As a solution to her fear of being alone, Charles had suggested she keep the door adjoining the rooms ajar. She had agreed.

She had agreed.

And that meant he could visit his son, who was no doubt, sleeping, and then take a quick look into the governess' room. Perhaps she was still awake. Perhaps she would agree to be the even number to tomorrow's informal dinner and dancing.

For some odd reason, he was inordinately stimulated just thinking about seeing Elaina again. Especially in her bed, in her nightclothes.

After reaching the top of the staircase, Charles turned to the left where his son... and Elaina now rested. If he had been dragged down by ennui before, now he was in roaring good spirits, indeed.

**✱ ✱ ✱ ✱**

Elaina had left a candle burning on her nightstand, but then as soon as she hit the pillow, she fell asleep. Totally out. But...

A creaking of the floorboards recalled her to the land of the living, at least temporarily. She might as well blow the candle out.

Rising up, she turned toward the nightstand to accomplish this action but then...

Oh good gosh, she saw the Duke! Her heart almost jumped out of her chest. He was still fully dressed in a navy blue tailcoat, light blue waistcoat, snowy white cravat, and beige trousers. His handsome face was barely lit but she could notice the sweep of his close-cut brown hair and his dark-as-the-devil eyes.

"Oh!" She patted at her heart to help it settle down. "What are you doing here?"

Sitting up she pulled the woolen blanket to cover her barely adequate nightgown.

His gaze focused exclusively on her as if... as if nothing else in the world existed.

"My apologies, Miss Wattell," he finally spoke. "I was visiting my son, saw that he was asleep, and then I thought of you, next door. I wanted to make certain you were comfortable in your new surroundings."

She fiddled with a loose strand of hair. Either it was very late or very early, but whatever the time, it was odd he wanted to check up on her now.

"Yes, thank you. Everything here is very nice." She had to focus her thoughts.

How weird it was having a conversation with a duke while she was in bed. It was a certainty Trudy wouldn't think this was... appropriate.

He took a step closer. "This bed is small."

"It's fine. Really. After all I'm only one person. A larger bed would take up too much of the room."

"Hmmn." His gaze was now restless, roaming over every available space on the bed and on her, even her hands, her neck, and her very messy bun.

Then he cleared his throat. "I did not have a chance to tell you about tomorrow, Miss Wattell. There will be a small foxhunt, my four friends and I will be the only hunters, and then for dinner, the Park shall be hosting two families that adjoin my lands. The Sinclairs and the MacLevys who, between them have five daughters of eligible age."

Well, that was interesting, but why did he feel he had to tell her this... now, in the middle of the night?

"One young woman," he continued, "is feeling poorly and will not be able to grace us with her presence."

Now Elaina curled the strand of hair around her finger. Talk about feeling awkward. She waited for him to get to the point of this... midnight interlude.

Still gazing down on her, he shifted position. "This defection leaves us one person, in particular, one female short." He inclined his head. "It would be my pleasure if you joined us for dinner and dancing."

Her eyes just about popped out of her head. "Me?" she squeaked. "I mean, I've never... dined in English society before. I'm not from here, you know. And dancing is totally out of the question. I have two left feet."

His eyebrows rose high on his forehead and he stared at the bed where her feet were covered.

"It's just an expression," she explained. "I don't dance well."

He nodded. "However, you *do* eat and you *can* carry a conversation, Miss Wattell. That is all that is required."

Joys.

Huffing a breath, she raised her gaze to his. "Well, okay. I'll do my best. I'll see if any of your mother's gowns can be quickly altered for me."

He placed his hands behind his back and walked up and down the very tiny space in the room that didn't have furniture cluttering it up. Stopping at the chest of drawers, he picked up her sunglasses and looked at them from every angle.

Her sunglasses were, of course, from the twenty-first century. A shiver ran down her spine.

"What are these?" he questioned.

"Glasses, or spectacles, to keep out the blinding light of the sun."

"Hmmn." He set them back down. "So, I caution you not to mention to my guests anything about your unusual circumstances or about cutting my hair. Haircutting is a trade, and ladies do not engage in trade."

La-di-da, again!

She flared her nostrils. "Are you sure you feel comfortable with me... and my *trade* background attending your extravagant party? I wouldn't want to be an... embarrassment."

How she managed to say that without slapping his hoity-toity face was a minor miracle!

"There is no need for you to be concerned, Miss Wattell. I have every confidence that you will deport yourself as a lady does."

Which meant he didn't consider her a lady! Ooh, her eyes now glowed fire-hot red. She was certain she could sear him to a crisp.

Then, he stepped closer to her position and... and had the audacity to sit at the foot of the bed.

Blinking, she then stared at him. She was, in a word, speechless.

He reached over and took her hand in his. "I am assured you will conduct yourself very properly, Miss Wattell, and your presence at the gathering will do me credit."

Okay, if she'd thought he'd had a Mount Vesuvius-type of anger about his misshapen hair, she felt that now she was Mount Vesuvius times ten. Times one hundred! She was *that* close to exploding. How dismissive he was. How holier-than-thou he was. How arrogant, conceited, and proud he was.

She took back her hand and gave him an artificial smile. "Actually, *Your Grace,* as I understand it, a man is not supposed to be in a woman's bedroom. Alone and behind closed doors? That's a compromising situation, isn't that right?"

Sitting stock still, he stared back at her.

"So, you see, you're in danger of ruining my reputation, *Your Grace.* Or maybe it's me, ruining your reputation? Either way, you need to leave... now."

He cleared his throat. "Those types of circumstances only apply to the upper class, Miss Wattell."

"Bullhockey! Men are men and women are women." Elaina waved her hand back and forth in between the space where they were both sitting. "As Miss Trundle would say, *'This is inappropriate.'* So very true."

He finally stood. "Miss Wattell--"

"I'll make a deal with you, *Your Grace.* I will attend your little haut ton gathering and I'll even be on my best 'civilized' behavior if..."

"If?" he repeated.

"If you refrain from visiting these rooms, especially if I happen to be in them." She lifted her eyebrow. "So, are we agreed?"

"Miss Wattell--"

"Are we agreed?"

His mouth worked but no words were forthcoming.

Actually that was quite amusing to watch. Cat must've gotten his tongue!

He inclined his handsome head. "Agreed. However, I had not intended--"

"Good-night, *Your Grace.*"

With his lips tightened, he made a small bow, and then left by way of Robbie's room.

Elaina sank back against her pillow. Phew. In her own way she felt as if she vanquished Jack In The Beanstalk's giant. Super. Now, all she had to do was calm herself down and get back to sleep.

# Chapter Seven

The official season of foxhunting started on the first of November, running through the beginning of May. It was one of the most complex and complicated bloodsports. As Charles had told his Pack, today's hunt would be more like a practice than anything else. He saw it as an excuse to gallop over fields and rolling hills.

There was no Master of the Hunt today, nor hunt followers--either by foot or on horses. There was only the five of them, along with servants, of course. As for costume, four vivid scarlet riding jackets with the obligatory brass hunt buttons were handed out to his guests, along with the customary black velvet huntcap.

The hounds chosen for today's hunt numbered only ten, but ten would certainly be enough to do the job. These varied dogs had been bred for stamina and their sense of smell. They were the best in all of East Sussex; they would run the fox to ground.

Charles and his Pack followed behind the hounds as they sniffed the grounds. Very soon the dogs would pick up the scent, and then the chase would be on.

Nome pulled his Arabian horse alongside Charles' dark as midnight stallion. "Wolfe, what ails you? You seem rather distracted. Aren't you looking forward to the hunt? I thought you always enjoyed this gentlemanly pursuit."

An accurate statement and an accurate assessment. Charles was, indeed, distracted. He could still imagine he smelled the floral scent of Elaina Wattell, most likely fresh from her bath last night. The feel of her soft hand in his, her dark hair coiled around in a bun, the flutter of her eyelashes against her cheeks...

She had been in a vulnerable position, made even more so by his unwelcome presence in her bedchamber. He had angered her, but as God was his witness, what had he said that was not the truth?

Holding the stallion's reins, he fisted his white-gloved hands. Her outraged expression returned to him, and then his previous thoughts returned to him as well. *No one took advantage of his servants,* he had decided self-righteously when Nome inquired about having his way with the female maids.

And yet, that was exactly what Charles had been doing last night. He had deliberately entered Elaina's bedchamber when she had been fast asleep. He conversed with her, he sat on her bed, he took her warm-from-sleep hand in his.

Without a doubt, he had no idea of what he had been thinking.

Then again, maybe he did. Perhaps, to his eternal detriment, he had seduction on his mind.

Blast him to the very devil!

He was a noble duke, one of the highest personages in the land. Elaina was... truthfully, at the moment he did not know what exactly she was, however she was now his son's governess. She was under his protection. He was a gentleman; she *deserved* his protection.

What kind of contemptible knave was he?

"Wolfe?" Nome leaned forward to tug on Charles' sleeve. "What is it? What is the matter? I daresay I'm quite alarmed now."

Fortunately, the hounds caught the fox's scent. With a volley of barking, the dogs dashed ahead as they followed the trail.

Charles urged his stallion in pursuit. He spoke over his shoulder. "A temporary megrim, Nome. My thanks for your concern, but it is nothing of consequence. Come, the chase is on. Let us give our steeds their heads and gallop like the wind after the hounds."

Perhaps this activity could erase his ignoble behavior from his mind.

**✳ ✳ ✳ ✳**

As soon as Elaina woke up, she sat up and threw back the blanket. Next, she set her bare feet on the wall-to-wall checked carpet. The room had a chill, so she wrapped up in the fuzzy robe Trudy had provided.

Elaina took a moment to orient herself: today was Saturday--the start of the weekend--so there was no need to pursue a traditional class setting with her new student. What she did have to worry about was getting a dinner party type of gown and then be on her best behavior with people who most likely were born with silver spoons in their mouths.

She wrinkled her nose just picturing it.

How the evening would go, she had no idea. If she could view the gathering as an amusing bit of fluff, that probably would be for the best.

She walked over to the large window, pushed aside the drapes, and then looked outside. Beautifully shaped hedges, delicate flowers providing color commentary among the greenery on the grounds, intricate statuary... this was the view in the front of the mansion. Perhaps she and Robbie could take a stroll about the gardens and identify the plant life.

For some reason, she was disappointed not to see any evidence of the foxhunt that the Duke had mentioned, although why she was disappointed, she had no idea.

Turning away from the window, she sighed. How strange to be settling into a completely different routine than the one she was used to for years. By rights she should've been out of her mind with worry about being thrown back two centuries in time. But no, instead, what was she doing? Thinking about being a teacher, a governess, to the son of a duke.

How very, very bizarre.

The Duke himself, Charles Burnley... well, he disturbed her on so many levels. He excited her; he infuriated her; he made her heart twitch in such an odd way. Why, she tingled even now just remembering what had happened last night.

What was wrong with her? Did she have some kind of Stockholm syndrome, where captives developed a psychological bond with their captors?

Not that he was her captor. Not that she fancied herself connected with him. Not that she was in love with him.

No, no, no. A thousand times no.

She wasn't a captive here, at least not yet. She'd try Robbie's brilliant notion that she visit the village healer. Maybe that woman could somehow duplicate whatever conditions were responsible for Elaina's inconvenient time-travel.

A knock at the door leading out into the corridor brought her focus back to the here-and-now.

Elaina opened the door to see a rejuvenated Trudy. The woman looked far less tired than she had yesterday. Having a smile on one's face could do that to a person.

"*Mademoiselle* Elaina." Trudy curtsied. "I'm here to help you dress."

Elaina opened the door wider. "C'mon in! You're just the person I want to see."

As soon as Trudy was inside, Elaina then stepped over to glance into Robbie's bedroom. The boy was still asleep with one arm flung over his head, and the other hand holding his teddy bear.

So cute!

She turned to Trudy. "Listen, I know this sounds odd, but I need a nice gown for tonight's dinner. Something that'll fit me and make me, you know, fashionable. The Duke wants me there to even out the numbers for the party."

Trudy's crescent-shaped eyes grew round. "Indeed? Indeed?" She patted at her slender breast. "While 'tis true the dowager's gowns are available, the designs are for, if I may be allowed, a mature woman."

Elaina heaved a heavy sigh. That was exactly what she thought.

"However," Trudy piped up, "a few of the Duchess of Wolfeshire's gowns are still on the premises. Locked away, I believe."

The lady's maid zipped over to the wardrobe. "Let us get you prepared for the day, and then we shall seek out Mr. Doyle. He knows where everything is at the Park, even ladies' clothing. With any good fortune, we may find the perfect gown for you, *Mademoiselle* Elaina, in a half-mourning shade that will not require many alterations.

"Good. That sounds super. Why don't you pick out something casual for now while I leave a message for Robbie?"

With Trudy busy, Elaina grabbed a pencil and paper. She wasn't sure if the boy would miss her when he woke up. He might kick up a fuss, so why take a chance? She wrote the note using block lettering, not cursive--after all she didn't know how well he could read or write.

She jotted down that she was seeing Mr. Doyle about some clothes, and then suggested the two of them could meet in the Breakfast Room for, well, breakfast.

Trudy worked her magic, dressing Elaina in a pinafore-type of day dress, with three quarter length sleeves, along with an updo of hair. The gown swam on her but Elaina didn't care. Quietly entering Robbie's room, she slipped the note under his teddy bear.

Now she was ready to talk with Mr. Doyle. Maybe he'd even know the name of that village healer.

**\* \* \* \***

It didn't take long to locate the butler. Trudy led Elaina straight to the Breakfast Room and that was where Mr. Doyle was, fussing with the table's place settings. The table had six chairs around it, but only two chairs had plates and utensils. Obviously, the Duke's guests had breakfasted earlier.

They both entered the room, but Trudy made her way in first and stood in front of the big man. She bobbed a curtsy.

"Mr. Doyle! Mr. Doyle! *Mademoiselle* Elaina and I have an urgent request only you can help us with. 'Tis relating to the late duchess' wardrobe."

The woman then lowered her gaze and a soft blush spread on her hollow cheeks.

Elaina blinked her surprise. She hadn't realized--then again, how could she have?--Trudy Trundle was attracted to the butler.

Mr. Doyle straightened his shoulders, cleared his throat, and then smoothed down his uniform's white collar.

Those were male preening gestures. So he returned Trudy's interest?

Elaina bit back a smile. How very, very sweet!

After first looking at Trudy, he then turned his gaze on Elaina. "May I infer that this request has something to do with His Grace's invitation for you to join tonight's dinner party, *Mademoiselle* Elaina?"

"Exactly." That he knew about tonight made things easier for her. She took a deep inhale. "I told the Duke that I've never... participated in this kind of formal English dinner, but he insisted. Something about having even numbers at the table. Anyway, I know I'd feel better about this if I could wear a striking dress."

Mr. Doyle made an avuncular smile. "I understand completely, *Mademoiselle* Elaina. 'To do battle with the enemy, one must take the greatest of care with the armor.'" He cleared his throat again. "A quote I once heard."

She had to laugh. "That describes it perfectly! Yes, I definitely will feel more prepared if I'm wearing the proper armor."

He inclined his great head. "Just so, *Mademoiselle*. Since time is of the essence in this matter, I shall have Mrs. Riddles accompany Trundle and me at once to the upper levels. The housekeeper has the key to the trunk containing the Duchess' attire."

Turning to Trudy, he then lowered his usually booming voice. "Then, Trundle, you may then remove whichever gowns you feel are best suited for *Mademoiselle* Elaina."

Elaina shot a glance at Trudy. Her rate of breathing noticeably increased!

The butler then looked at Elaina. "Also, you should be aware, *Mademoiselle,* His Grace has sent his valet to London with the express purpose of procuring a new wardrobe for you. His Grace understood that you... were deficient in that area and he wishes you to feel comfortable in your duties as governess to Master Robert."

With that bombshell, Mr. Doyle bowed and Trudy curtsied, and they both left the Breakfast Room.

Elaina pulled out a chair and plopped herself down. Oh good gosh, how did she feel about that? As she understood rules for proper and above reproach behavior, men weren't supposed to buy women clothing. In these times, that was rather like being a kept woman.

Well, she certainly *wasn't* going to be the Duke's mistress... now or in the future.

Then again, she did need clothes. Glancing down at what she was wearing, that particular fact was glaringly obvious. The shapeless pinafore gown would probably scare anyone with a delicate sensibility.

Pooh. She wrinkled her nose. Who cared about that?

Getting up, she walked to the sideboard to pour herself a cup of coffee, and then returned to the table.

So, she had to be realistic; the deed was done; the valet was already in London. What was she worrying about? The Duke could certainly afford the expense. She'd accept the clothes as "payment" for her services as governess.

There. Her conscience was clear.

Taking a sip of black coffee, she waited for Robbie to join her for breakfast.

**\* \* \* \***

Hours later, Elaina drooped; she knew she did. She and Robbie had taken a tour of the great house at Wolfeshire Park to look at all the impressive... and expensive paintings, thereby cramming in an art history lesson. Then they wandered outside to peruse the many gardens dotted with flowers of every variety, even common daisies.

Robbie had insisted that she wear a bonnet--needed for propriety sake and to protect "delicate" skin from the sun. So she did. He had even worn a straw hat, too, for part of the time. Now he freely dashed about the fields with his curly brown hair flopping in the breeze.

He'd mentioned that he wanted her to cut his hair. Maybe she should remind him?

They jumped rope, or as he called it, skipping rope; they pushed around metal hoops with sturdy sticks; they played catch with a colorful ball; they even rushed about playing something called battledore and shuttlecock. This was a game more familiar to her as badminton.

Now, frankly, her energy was spent.

Sitting... or slumping... on a wooden bench set in a field of fine daisies to the back of the great house, she watched Robbie as he continued to zip around tall hedges decorating the grounds. He played some kind of made-up game, as if the day had just started instead of the day nearly being over.

"I'm so glad you're here, Elle," he huffed as he rounded another huge hedge. "A good 'un! The best! Fine as five pence! I'd give you more words if I could think of them."

As tired as she was, she had to smile. "That's okay, Robbie. I appreciate the two thumbs up. But we really need to call it a day now. I'm--"

"Good-O!" he interrupted. "I hear the hounds! They're back from the hunt. The stable is around the corner, Elle. I'm going to check them out. Be right back."

He raced away before she could give permission.

*Where does he get his get-up-and-go?* She shook her head. Oh to be seven again!

She heard the barking, too, so obviously Robbie was right about the foxhunt being over. Then she shrugged. This was his house; who was she to give permission for him to see the stables?

Trying to get off the bench so she could follow him, her legs refused to carry her weight. Oof! She fell back onto the wooden planks of the bench.

Oh well. She'd better just rest a moment and then she'd try again. She closed her eyes...

**\* \* \* \***

Atop his pure black stallion, Charles led his Pack's four horses over to the stables so the grooms could provide these prime goers with brisk rubdowns, large bags of barley-meal, and fresh hay to reward them for today's service. His friends had already returned to the house, no doubt to get their own massage, a refreshment or two, and, of course, a nap. All four of them had been fagged to death by the foxhunt. As Charles was as well, however as host, he had certain obligations.

Ten foxhounds stood around Charles by his horse's feet. The dogs were well-trained. They knew as soon as the horses were fed, that they would be next.

He dismounted, gave his stallion an affectionate pat on the flank, and then removed the trophy--the brush--from his saddle. After nodding at the groom to take the horse back to the stable, Charles held up the fox's tail. What the devil was he going to do with this?

In truth he never cared to kill the fox at the end of the hunt. Something rather barbaric about it, however Nome had insisted. The man must have had the sin of the bloodlust attached to him, in addition to actual lust.

Stepping around the barking hounds, he directed the remaining grooms to take care of the dogs. He then spotted Edgars, his grizzled head gardener, helping out with the smaller animals.

He called the gardener over. "Here is a bit of a coil, Edgars. Tell me, what the devil am I to do with this bloody trophy?"

About to hand over the blood-dripping tail, he heard his son's voice.

"Don't, Father." Robert walked over, very casually dressed, dirty, but happy. He confidently held out his hand. "Give it to me. I'll give the tail to Elle."

Perhaps some women found a bloody trophy agreeable. Although he did not know Elaina at all, somehow he did not believe she would be included in that group.

However, perhaps his son knew her better.

Charles handed over the brush. "As you wish, Son." He eyed the boy's unkempt appearance. "You look like a street urchin, Robert. Where is your esteemed governess? I wonder that she allows you to be seen in such a fashion."

"We've been playing for hours, sir. She's just around the corner by the hedges." The boy then turned to Edgars. "Remember how you always tell me there are no surprises in the gardens, Edgars? Well, you're wrong! I found one. I found a big surprise: Elle, my new governess!"

The head gardener raised his bushy eyebrows. "Hey now, Master Robert. Ye be saying a woman be wandering about in my gardens?"

Charles had to squelch inappropriate gossip. "There was some kind of a mistake, Edgars, however, all is taken care of. Come, Robert."

With his hand on his son's shoulder, Charles headed for the back of his great house. Truth be told, he looked forward to seeing Elaina again.

Rounding the corner, he saw her. There she sat, on a bench in a field of blooming daisies. But she could not have been awake; her head, with its straw bonnet askew, lolled over to her right shoulder. Her neck was crooked in an uncomfortable looking manner.

She wore some type of shapeless pinafore gown, black in color with loose semi-long sleeves in white. Her bonnet had seen better days as well; a few broken pieces of straw stuck up in places they did not belong.

Even as unfashionably dressed as the woman was, he found her very appealing. Her dark eyelashes fluttered ever so slightly, most likely in response to a dream. The soft curve of her rosy cheeks, the determined point of her chin, her lips shining with a peachy glow...

He inhaled slowly. Yes, she was a beauty.

Walking up to the bench, he feasted on the long line of her neck again. A fair amount of bare skin was exposed along her shoulder. He followed its path until the scoop of the gown hid that particular forbidden delight.

Perhaps his scrutiny was something she could feel for those thick lashes of hers fluttered once more, only this time she woke up.

"Oh!" She sat up and then straightened the neckline on her gown. "My apologies. I must have fallen asleep."

Before he had a chance to speak, Robert wagged that infernal tail in front of her. "Look, Elle! It's the prize. See how bushy it is!"

She glanced at it, then looked away. "Yes. Yes, it was a beautiful tail."

The boy then lifted his head to look at Charles. "How many hunters and hounds, Father? How many did it take to run down the fox?"

Charles adjusted the beak on his velvet huntcap. "There were five of us, along with ten hounds at the hunt."

With the brush in hand, Robert extended his arm toward Elaina. "Good-O. This is for you, Elle. Look, it even has a white tip on the end."

Her distinctive eyes widened as Robert moved the tail closer. "Thank you for thinking of me, but I tell you what. You keep it. I, um, to tell you the truth, I was rooting for the fox."

There were no hurt feelings on Robert's part. Swishing the tail in the air, he lunged forward and back with it as if it had been some type of sword.

As Charles brushed dirt from the sleeve of his scarlet riding jacket, he regarded her. "You disapprove of foxhunting, Miss Wattell?"

"Well, it's hardly 'sporting,' don't you think? I know it's not any of my business, but one small animal against ten dogs, five men, and five horses... the odds are certainly quite uneven." She shrugged. "Just an observation."

"An interesting point. I will grant you that." He held out his hand to help her up. "It is time to return to the house. I see Robert's nanny making her way out here to collect him. Teatime, I will wager. Robert never likes to miss the culinary delights of teatime."

Elaina eyed his outstretched hand and then slowly placed hers in his. For a moment, he curved his fingers around her palm, enjoying the feel of her. In that moment, she stood, and quickly removed her hand from his.

Then Nanny Price hurried over, huffing and puffing. She stood in front of Charles and bowed. "Your Grace, 'tis time for Master Robert's tea."

The poor woman's matronly bosom quivered as she caught her breath and her frizzy grey locks of hair stood at attention in the gentle breeze. Frankly, she looked every one of her sixty-odd years.

He had a sudden thought. Perhaps Price's days as a nanny should be ended. Perhaps she should retire from her duties and live on the estate without worries. Yes, he would discuss this with Doyle.

"Come, Robert," he called to his son. "Price is here to take you back to the house. You need to clean up and dress accordingly."

The boy stomped over to him and Elaina, and then raised a woebegone face. "But I want Elle to come, too."

Elaina stepped forward and gave the boy a hug. Charles noted she took care to avoid the fox's tail.

"But of course I'm going inside, Rob-Robert. I need to get cleaned up, too. I would just like to talk with your father, if he has a minute? So you go on ahead with Mrs. Price."

"Sure." Robert smiled up at her then turned around, heading for the house.

Price leaned toward Charles, whispering in her shaky voice, "Sir, I am in alt that *Mademoiselle* Elaina has accepted the governess position. 'Tis the very thing. Why, Master Robert is like a changed boy."

The two of them, a small boy and a frazzled frump of a woman made their way back to one of Wolfeshire Park's rear entrances.

The image of Elaina giving his needy son a motherly embrace teased at Charles. Would that she would do the very same thing to him, only, of course, not a motherly embrace. Shaking away his unsuitable thoughts, he extended his hand in the direction of the house and waited for her to begin walking.

"I do have a few minutes, Miss Wattell. What would you like to discuss with me?"

She walked alongside him at a sedate pace. "Well, first, I just want to make sure you really want me to join your guests for dinner."

"In truth, I am looking forward to it." He then raked his gaze over her dowdy gown. "I hope you have something more fitting for tonight's formalities."

"I do. I hope you don't mind, but Trudy selected something from your wife's wardrobe. She and Fannie are altering the gown now."

He lifted an eyebrow. "Trudy?"

"Trudy Trundle. Your mother's lady's maid. I hope it's not... forward of me to have her help me."

"No, Miss Wattell. It is not forward of you at all. I am assured it is entirely proper."

She huffed a sigh. "Good. I mean, Trudy was worried about being let go since... well, there's been no need of a lady's maid since your mother passed away."

Charles nodded. "I should have made that clear to Trundle. She is to continue here at Wolfeshire Park. So, of course, she may serve you as a lady's maid."

When they reached the back entrance into the house, Elaina placed her small hand on his lower arm and smiled at him.

By the good Lord above, that unaffected smile burrowed deep into his heart.

"Thank you." She made a graceful curtsy. "That means a lot to Trudy."

One of the footmen opened the door. She thanked him and stepped over the threshold.

Then she turned to Charles. "So, as you see, I'm in desperate need of a bath. If I'm going to be ready for your formal dinner party, I'd better hustle."

And she did. Before he could even blink his eyes, she was gone.

He glanced down in the direction that she had disappeared. As he had told her earlier, he *was* looking forward to seeing her at dinner. He was *excessively* looking forward to seeing her, and perhaps even dancing with her.

For the first time in many months, Charles smiled without restraint.

# Chapter Eight

Despite being tired and achy from her very active day, Elaina still had a lot of energy. After she bathed and dried her hair, she was on hold on what she should do next until the alterations on her evening dress were finished.

Pacing around her bedroom proved to be difficult with two other people present, so she fidgeted instead. She *had* to have something to do.

As Trudy handled the extra hemming on tonight's attire: a grey crêpe gown over a black silk slip, Fannie finished re-sewing the jet beads lining the gown's top and around the bodice. But now, since her job was over, the little housemaid sat on her heels and looked up at Elaina.

"'Tis a lovely dress, *Mademoiselle*. Without a doubt you'll be the prettiest lady tonight. All the gents won't be able t'take their eyes off you." Blinking, Fannie twirled one of her greasy brown curls around her finger.

"'Tis a certainty, *Mademoiselle*. You are, as the French say, *très chic*," Trudy mumbled as she had a mouthful of straight pins in her mouth.

Elaina held out her hand to help Fannie from the floor. "Ladies, please. Call me Elaina, okay? At least when we're alone."

Taking a pin from her mouth to insert it into the material, Trudy mumbled again. "If you wish it. I shall certainly try... Elaina."

Then it was the bashful housemaid's turn. She blushed and brushed that lock of dirty hair back into her cotton mob cap. "I, too, will try... Elaina."

And that gave Elaina an idea. "Fannie, I need you to be my guinea pig."

That thought made her freeze in her tracks. Just a couple of days ago she had referred to her friend, Leila, as a guinea pig.

She blinked her distress away and pulled the little maid into the bathroom area.

"Guinea pig?" Fannie's light brown eyes nearly popped out of her head. "Whatever does that mean?"

"It means I'm going to experiment on you... with a shampoo I made. But don't worry. I already used it on my hair." She fluffed out the sides of her hair. "See? Nice and bouncy. Smells so good, too."

Fannie darted her gaze about the room as if she was going to be tortured. "Oh, I dinna know. I--"

"*I* know. Trust me." Elaina sat her friend down on a stool in the hip bath. "You and Trudy are helping me; fixing me up tonight so hopefully, I won't fall flat on my face. I really appreciate this. Plus, Fannie, you were so kind as to take me in as a roommate two nights ago. Honestly, I just want to return the favor."

Pulling off Fannie's cotton mob cap, Elaina then played with the maid's curled-in-the-front, shoulder-length hair. Hmmn. She could do something nice with this hair.

"Okay, I've got my hair supplies and the shampoo bottle. All you have to do is take a deep breath, relax, lean back, and I'll wet your head."

Truthfully, she was dying to get her fingers into Fannie's wild curls. Elaina had a weird fascination with hair. Honestly, she was probably born that way. Once a hairstylist, always a hairstylist.

With a big smile on her face, she proceeded to work her magic.

A duke's estate was, by necessity, large. Wolfeshire Park was no different. A vast estate and a vast amount of servants with which to service it. Naturally, Charles' servants could easily handle the numbers for tonight's dinner party--fourteen. The quantity of guests was a mere drop in the bucket compared with some of the gala events Wolfeshire Park had housed in the past.

Fourteen for dinner and also for dancing.

The entire party--save one--waited in the Blue Velvet Salon adjoining the State Dining Room. As host, Charles dutifully mingled among his guests. His visitors were of three groups: the older, married group; the unattached ladies; and the unattached gentlemen.

At present he was socializing with the married males. The married females were interspersed with the younger ladies and gentlemen.

Elaina Wattell was, of course, the guest not present. She was not late-- not yet--however he did find himself impatiently watching the white paneled double doors for her entrance. If he was truthful with himself, he could admit to his heart beating a little faster than usual.

"Jolly good foxhunt you arranged for today, Wolfe." Lambert Sinclair, the neighbor to the west, lifted his brandy snifter as a greeting, and then winked. "Heard the hounds outside from my rose gardens."

"Today was a practice hunt, Sinclair." Charles raised his own snifter, but his reason was to take a sip. "Something to pass the time until the start of the season in November."

"I heard the hounds, as well." Vernon MacLevy, neighbor to the north, was not to be outdone. "Feel free to run your hounds on my property, Wolfe. Let the dogs roam free. To be sure, run them anytime at all."

Then MacLevy raised his own brandy snifter, albeit a little late. He not only raised it, but took a healthy gulp of French brandy. Then another, and another, and then he was in need of a refill.

Charles withheld his smile. The MacLevys and the Sinclairs had been competitors since the time of King Henry VIII. At this point in time, the issue that seemed to be on both fathers' minds was which one of their daughters would secure the best alliance... and not only that, but which daughter would be the first to the altar.

MacLevy had beat Sinclair in the number of progeny: three. Sinclair had beat MacLevy in the amount of dowry to offer prospective suitors.

Sinclair wiped at his forehead with a linen handkerchief. "It is so unfortunate my youngest, Constance, couldn't be here tonight, Wolfe. The dear girl cried, but..." He shrugged his round shoulders. "Female troubles, you know."

MacLevy couldn't wait to jump in. "My three are as fit as a fiddle. Faith, Hope, and Charity, don't you know?"

Charles sighed. Obviously, given names were another area with which to compete. Constance Sinclair's older sister was named Prudence.

After glancing at the ormolu clock on the fireplace mantel, he glanced at the double doors once again, and then turned to his neighbors. "As soon as Constance is feeling more the thing, we can arrange another get-together."

Giving the men a nod, he moved toward the larger group of four ladies, four gentlemen, and two mothers. The mothers seemed to be bickering about something among themselves, echoing their husbands' mode of conversing.

The young ladies were fine examples of the Fair Sex, simpering away like a gaggle of pea-gooses. The Misses MacLevy all resembled each other with silver blonde hair, pale blue eyes, and a bit long in their faces. They looked so much alike, Charles could admit to always being confused as to which one was Faith, Hope, or Charity. Only eighteen months apiece separated them, from the eldest to the next to the youngest.

Prudence Sinclair, however, was a Diamond of the first water, with a generous smile, turned up nose, and a twinkle in her hazel eyes. In addition, she had personality.

Nome edged out the other bachelors and was, of course, stationed next to Miss Sinclair.

Charles turned his attention back to the double doors. It was almost time to proceed into the State Dining Room. Where was Elaina? She had not changed her mind about joining the dinner party... had she?

The Arabian-styled doors edged in alabaster vividly contrasted against the Bishop's blue of the painted walls. For just a moment, the whimsical fashion of this architecture spurred him on to imagine himself as a sultan, with Elaina as a new prize to his harem. She would dance for him, and only for him, wearing fluttering scarves hiding and revealing her curvy womanly body...

Hmmn. He enjoyed that moment; he enjoyed it very much.

At last the doors opened. Doyle entered in his decidedly grand manner, gave a slight bow, and announced, "*Mademoiselle* Elaina Wattell."

And then, she walked into the Blue Velvet Salon.

And then, Charles felt a shift within him. He stood stone-like, entranced, even mesmerized. She was like a breeze on a summer's day--deliciously fresh with a touch of sultriness in her air. To his practiced eye, she wore no cosmetics to cover her flawless complexion, nor blackened soot to heighten the curve of her brown and green eyes. Her chestnut hair shone with golden highlights and was pleasingly curled around her handsome face.

His gaze dipped lower. Her graceful neck stood exposed, calling attention to itself without benefit of an expensive necklace. And if he was not mistaken, a pulse point twitched furiously next to one of her unadorned earlobes.

His gaze continued to descend. The pleasing décolletage revealed perfectly rounded breasts... and in response to that tempting sight, his hands by his sides stretched out as if to begin their assault on such fair beauty.

The French grey crêpe gown with sheer puffed sleeves had been worn by his late wife, however to be truthful, she had never graced it in such a fashion as Elaina Wattell.

No. He grit his teeth to recall himself. He could not dwell on these improper thoughts. He was the host; he had to remember that and act accordingly.

He walked over to her and bowed. "Miss Wattell. I am pleased you could join us tonight."

Once again he glanced at her face. That she wore no cosmetics was important to him, especially in view of how his wife had died.

She gave a quick curtsy. "I'm sorry I'm late, sir. Your son wanted..." She paused as if phrasing her words. "He wanted me to remain with him. I had to offer a bribe."

"A bribe? What would induce a lad of seven to behave? Except for a punishment, of course."

She shrugged, which inadvertently called attention to her perfect bosom. "I told him that if the weather cooperated tomorrow, we could swim in the lake to cool off."

At such an unexpected answer, Charles blinked. Then the image of her wearing a bathing dress... or not wearing anything at all blasted through him. For once, he was at a loss for words.

It was then that the fastidiously dressed Lord Nome accosted them.

"Saving the best for last, are you, Wolfe?" Nome made a formal bow. "*Mademoiselle,* I am delighted to make your acquaintance. I am Alastair

Dover, the Earl of Nome, at your service."

She darted a glance at Charles and then performed her curtsy. "And I'm Elaina Wattell, sir."

Nome raised his rakish gaze to focus on her face. "Say the word, *Mademoiselle,* and allow me to be your devoted gallant."

Although Charles' name was Wolfe--Wolfeshire--it seemed Nome took over the meaning of the word "wolf." His blazing blue eyes were piercing in intensity, and his mouth... when he smiled, his teeth looked overly sharp.

Charles wanted to floor the man. Instead, he schooled himself to watch Elaina's reaction to this out-and-outer.

A sweet smile lifted her lips... and that caused Charles' heart to sink.

"I thank you for your kindness, sir," she replied in her dulcet voice. "But I have no need of a gallant."

"No need? Intriguing," Nome murmured.

"An effective set-down," Charles mumbled.

Flaring his nostrils at his so-called friend, he then raised his voice to the room at large. "Let us adjourn to the State Dining Room and there, after we are seated we shall perform the introductions."

Next came the tedious entry into the dining room according to rank. He had Mrs. Sinclair on his arm; not that she outranked Mrs. MacLevy. Doyle always kept track of whom Charles had escorted in at the previous social gathering. Tonight it was Mrs. Sinclair's turn for the privilege.

Mrs. MacLevy was with Nome. Miss Prudence Sinclair entered with Lord Martiz. Miss Faith MacLevy was on Lord Otto's arm. Miss Hope MacLevy came in with her father, Mr. MacLevy. Miss Charity MacLevy entered with Mr. Sinclair. And Elaina had the good fortune to be on Jules Greensby's arm. Or rather, Greensby had the good fortune to escort Elaina.

Charles envied the man.

Inside the pretentiously grand State Dining Room, Charles stood to the side while his footmen helped the guests to their assigned chairs. The East Indian rosewood table was set for fourteen, seven on each side. Once everyone was comfortably seated, Charles leaned over to place his hand on the back of the empty chair at the head of the table.

He explained, "You will notice that I am not sitting at the head of the table as is usual, but here, at the end next to Mrs. MacLevy, and across from Mrs. Sinclair. The reason for this departure from tradition is that my dear mother, Anastasia, would always sit at the opposite end of the table from me. As her departure from this good Earth is recent, I wish to honor her in this way, as if she were still at the end of the table, leading us on to dinner."

Many murmurs drifted upwards towards the elaborately painted ceiling in the Blue Velvet Salon. Most were favorable comments, however at least one was not.

Mr. MacLevy had the temerity to utter, "P-Positively morbid! I s-say, a deuced too sen... sentimental f-for my t-tastes."

It was a certainty the man was already a bit bosky, three sheets in the wind.

Mrs. MacLevy had the good sense to blush. Obviously her husband's tactless words embarrassed her. Or perhaps it was his muzzy condition.

As Charles seated himself next to the woman, he glanced down to the end of the table diagonally across from him. It was there that Elaina sat, next to Mr. Sinclair and across from Greensby.

Once again he envied Greensby's close proximity to Elaina. However, he would have his opportunity to speak with her and be next to her once the dancing began.

Would that this tedious dinner be over as quickly as possible!

He signaled Doyle to begin serving the first course, and then proceeded to perform the introductions.

Elaina had to be honest; after she steered the conversation away from her, she actually enjoyed conversing with her dinner companions. Mr. Sinclair, seated to her left, was an amusing country gentleman, however what was really funny was that after everything he said, the other country gentleman, Mr. MacLevy on the other side of the table, would engage in some type of one-upmanship... in addition to Mr. MacLevy being embarrassingly drunk.

She also enjoyed conversing with Jules Greensby, across the table from her. He told her, quite frankly, too, that he was only a plain mister among these squires, lords, viscounts, earls, and dukes.

"Rich as Croesus," he had confided. "Whomever Croesus was." Then he gave a titter of a laugh.

"Obviously he was a very wealthy man," Elaina put in her own two cents. "A man so rich, he became a myth and the standard of prosperity."

Maybe her comment pleased Mr. Greensby because he gazed at her with his turquoise blue eyes and then nodded. "Just so! Just so."

Mr. Greensby even leaned over to Mr. MacLevy after one of his obnoxious remarks, and told him to "Stuff it!"

All in all, Elaina didn't disgrace herself. Or at least, she didn't think she had. The dinner was delicious; Mrs. Parsons, the cook, outdid herself. But now dinner was over and dancing would begin in the Blue Velvet Salon.

Standing in this blue-themed room, she thought it a little narrow to dance, but as the two older men refused to take to the floor, along with Mrs. MacLevy, and Mrs. Sinclair offering to play the pianoforte, there were only ten people who would be partaking of this amusement.

Elaina smiled. Matchmaking, Regency style.

As the first dance was a kind of line dance or country dance, she gave her regrets to Lord Nome, who had wished to partner with her.

Lord Nome was a very handsome man, and he knew it, too. A frown lingered on his plump lips and then he bowed and made his elegant way over to Prudence Sinclair. He was fortunate that she agreed.

The music began and the dance started with two lines--four young ladies on one side and four fashionable gentlemen on the other. For a moment Elaina watched as the ladies and men whirled and twirled up and down the wooden floor.

The room looked so stylish with all these lovely young people moving gracefully, she couldn't help but deepen her smile.

"You are smiling, Miss Wattell," came a deep voice over her right shoulder. "Dare I hope you approve of these entertainments?"

It was the Duke, of course. Other than the older couples, he was the only one not on the dance floor.

She raised her gaze to meet his dark eyes. "It's good to see people having fun."

The Duke looked particularly handsome tonight. His suit jacket was made of black kerseymere with claw-hammer tails and dazzling silver buttons. The jacket was open to show his celestial blue silk waistcoat and intricately tied cravat. Black breeches, white hose, and black silk pumps completed his attire. Truthfully, he was as gorgeous as a dream.

And when he raked his gaze over her, her breasts tingled in response.

"May I have the honor of your hand for the next set, Miss Wattell?" He inclined his head as he asked.

"Oh. I... um, no. I think I told you I don't know how to dance, so actually, it's best if I just retire for the night. Honestly, I've had quite a day."

He lifted an eyebrow. "As I recall, you stated you don't dance well, especially with your two left feet. That is different than not being able to dance at all."

He dropped his gaze to the floor and at her black silk slippers. "For two left feet, they look rather charming."

She tapped one foot. "Look, it all means the same thing. I've carried out my part in this arrangement, *Your Grace*. I ate, I spoke with your guests. And now I'm saying my goodbyes." She shrugged. "Running around all day with a seven-year-old is pretty tiring."

"For your *advanced* years." His lips twitched. "Four and twenty, if I recall correctly."

The closest dancer to them--Mr. Greensby tripped and thereby stumbled into Elaina. He apologized profusely, and she patted his arm and smiled at him.

Once the ungainly Mr. Greensby had lumbered off, she turned to Charles and wrinkled her nose at him. "You recall correctly. So now you can do your minuets, country dances, quadrilles, cotillions, whatever, without me to gum up, um, mess up the works."

Turning toward the exit door, she was stopped by his warm hand on her upper arm. Bare skin on bare skin. She had to stifle her shiver.

"The next dance will be a waltz, Miss Wattell. Surely you can waltz. If not, I will be honored to guide you."

She opened her mouth to protest, but he had the audacity to place his index finger on her lips.

Ooh! Who knew lips could tingle, too?

"Grant me this, Miss Wattell. One waltz, and then you may retire."

Pulling away from his potent touch, she huffed out a breath. "Promise?"

His smile actually warmed her through and through. "Yes, I do."

"Well, okay."

She supposed she didn't really have a choice. After all, she was a freeloader, mooching off of his largess.

Just then, the dancers made their styled bows to signal the end of the set. At the pianoforte, Mrs. Sinclair paused, changed the sheets of music, and then set her fingers on the keys to play a lively triple-time beat.

A triple-time beat signified a waltz. The Duke had been correct about the next dance.

There was a bit of a scramble as guests changed partners. But of course, the Duke was right there beside her. He extended his hand out to her, palm up.

So formal! With a little roll of her eyes, Elaina then placed her hand in his.

Swell. Now she would have to manage being so close to him, breathing in his masculine scented air, and dealing with the sensation of his firm hand around her waist.

# Chapter Nine

At the start of the waltz, Charles bowed to Elaina's curtsy. He took a deep breath and then curved his right arm around her tiny waist, and with his left, he held her right hand. Settling her near him but not against him, he again breathed in the scent of her floral perfume.

This was it; this was what he had been waiting for all day. Perhaps ever since meeting her. Had it been just yesterday? The day before? Indeed, he almost felt that he had known her for the whole of his life.

She swayed sweetly in time with the music, and responded smoothly to his movements. He enjoyed that power, that she moved as he moved. The feel of her in his arms created an overpowering yearning, that and her floral fragrance stirred something primal within him.

He was not used to such primitive sensations. He felt untamed, out of control.

To the sound of the pianoforte music, they glided along the flooring in the Blue Velvet Salon. The sound and feel of Elaina's increased breathing lit a fire deep into his soul. And the sight of her flushed face so close to his caused him to tighten his hold on her... an inappropriate action on his part, true.

Sound, touch, sight, smell... as for her taste... perhaps later tonight he could sample her honey.

Smiling, he enjoyed the feel of her warm breath against his ear.

"You are holding me too close, *Your Grace*. Your friend, Lord Nome, is scowling at you."

Charles turned her away from Nome. "Devil take him. Perhaps he does not appreciate his partner, Miss Faith MacLevy, as I appreciate you."

He then swung Elaina around as they reached the back of the salon and lessened his hold on her.

"Dancing with you is extremely agreeable, Miss Wattell. I would say you waltz very well, indeed. No two left feet for you," he murmured against the shell of her ear.

"You are too kind." She moved her head back, away from his. "Your guests seem to be having a good time. From what I see, Lord Otto is enamored by his partner, Prudence Sinclair."

"Yes, she is the eldest Sinclair chit." Charles tugged Elaina in a little closer. "Whether Otto is thunderstruck by her beauty or her dowry is certainly unknown."

She gave him a frown. "I take that back. You are *most* unkind, to your friend and to Miss Sinclair. She's a very charming young woman."

*Not as charming as you,* he wanted to say, however he restrained himself. "I daresay she is."

He took a moment to glance at the other dancers. "Here is Lord Martiz twirling about with the blushing Miss Hope MacLevy. Proper. Very Proper. And now for Mr. Greensby. Poor fellow, he appears to be treading on Miss Charity MacLevy's toes."

"He's a nice man," Elaina commented. "I like him."

"Do you?" Charles executed a rough turn that then caused her to bump against him. "Or is it his money you like?"

Sighing, she shook her head. "Crude, cynical, and uncalled for. You should have your knuckles rapped."

He smiled. "I have not had my knuckles rapped in quite some time. Would you care to take on the task?"

"I'll pass." She looked over his shoulder at the pianoforte. "The waltz should be over by now."

"Not if Mrs. Sinclair has a tendency... or a request to repeat the music."

Elaina's lips tightened but she did not reply.

He had to get her talking. He needed to learn more about her. "I find I do not know much about you... Elaina, if I may."

She fluttered her eyelashes. "Will I still have to call you *Your Grace?*"

In truth, she still should address him thusly, however the connection between them was so strong--the strongest he had felt in quite some time.

He inclined his head. "Charles will do."

"Will it?" She threw back her head and laughed.

In that moment he completely inhaled the sight of her long, beautiful neck and upraised chin.

"What about Charlie? Or Chuck? Or, I know... Chas?" Her playful laughter rang out over the dying chords on the pianoforte.

To punish her, he pressed her tighter against him, so tight he could feel the soft mounds of her breasts now flattened against his chest.

"Charles, m'dear, only Charles. You will remember that, yes?"

Before she had a chance to push him away, the waltz ended, so he took a step from her.

He bowed. "We shall have to do this again sometime, Elaina. Sometime soon."

When she skewed her lips, he had to chuckle. He had never met such a delightful female.

Just as chatter from the guests now filled the salon, the double doors opened and in rushed... a housemaid... Fannie, he believed. Her servant's gown was ripped at the neckline, her mop cap was hanging off her head; she was in a jumble of disarray but for her shining, wavy, sweet-smelling hair. Its dazzling color reminded him of a tawny breeze. Without a doubt, Elaina must have had a hand in the hair's transformation.

Unfortunately, in her rush to enter, Fannie barreled into Greensby, who steadied the maid, and then stared at her in amazement.

Elaina reacted quickly. She hurried over and curved her arm about the maid's shoulders. "What happened, Fannie?" Are you all right?"

"Oh, *Mademoiselle!* Beggin' your pardon. I beg everyone's pardon. I'm so sorry, but... but 'tis Master Robert. He suddenly woke up and just flew into the boughs. He thrashed about, calling for you. Put Nanny and me into a fair pucker. We tried t'calm him but he won't be soothed. He needs t'see you, *Mademoiselle.* He demands t'see you."

Stepping in front of the maid, Charles gestured toward her ripped bodice. He thundered, "My son did this to you?"

Fannie's lips wobbled. "He dinna mean it, Your Grace. He just be wild, throwin' himself this way and that."

This was unacceptable behavior. That his son, the future Duke of Wolfeshire, attacked a servant...

In truth, Charles was horrified.

"Come," he commanded, gesturing toward Elaina and Fannie. He then gave his apologies to his guests. "Continue the festivities without me. I shall be back shortly."

With a stride as fast as he could go, he took the grand staircase with both women following behind him.

**✳ ✳ ✳ ✳**

Lifting the crêpe material of her gown, Elaina hurried to follow the Duke's footsteps. She knew, without a doubt, that Mount Vesuvius was about to blow... again. How could she calm him down and also his son?

Robbie was the easy one; he'd obviously had a nightmare, and he woke up afraid. To lash out against Fannie, though, was not to be permitted.

He'd kicked up a fuss before dinner, too. That was why Elaina had been late getting to the Blue Velvet Salon. What could she do to help him recover from the loss of his mother and his grandmother? He was so fixated on her, but honestly, she couldn't stay here. If there was any way of getting back to her own time, she was taking it.

She shivered. She *was* taking it.

The Duke reached Robbie's door and then turned around to look at Elaina and Fannie. "You both will remain here until I send for you." His voice was as cold as the grave.

Fannie bobbed a curtsy, but Elaina just stared at him. Gone was the charming dancer who held her in his arms too tightly, who whispered in her ear, who suggested another waltz at another time.

No. This man had narrowed eyes, a clenched jaw, a stiff poker stance, and fisted hands.

Her heart thudded with dread. Oh good gosh, she feared for Robbie.

As he grabbed the door handle, she placed her hand on his upper arm, inadvertently feeling his taut bicep muscle through the tailcoat's sleeve. "You... You'll go easy on him, won't you?"

As he gazed at her, his eyes narrowed even further. "That is not your concern, madam." Then he entered the bedroom and shut the door.

The next second, Nanny Price and Mrs. Riddles were ejected into the hallway. Well, to be truthful, they rushed out on their own steam.

"Tush!" The housekeeper patted at her matronly chest. "I have never seen His Grace in such a froth."

"Oh my eyes!" the nanny added. "Wot will we do? Wot will we do?"

Panic had a way of spreading, so Elaina had to take charge. At least, she felt she had to take charge.

"Ladies, what did the Duke tell you? Are you also to wait for him? He wants Fannie and me to remain here."

Mrs. Riddles briskly shook her head. "Tsk-tsk. No. Nanny and I are to repair to our bedchambers for the night, *Mademoiselle* Elaina. However, you Fannie, His Grace declared you shall have tomorrow all to yourself. You may go into town if you wish, gel."

Fannie slapped her hands on her pinkened cheeks. "As I live and breathe!"

As soon as the older ladies left, Fannie leaned closer to Elaina. "I dinna know what t'make of this. A whole day t'myself! I dinna know what I should do."

The answer to that was easy. "Do whatever you want, Fannie. Relax, stroll about the gardens, take a ride to town, read a book--"

"I canna read, Elaina. 'Tis somethin' I've always wanted t'learn."

"Don't worry, I'll teach you. You probably know how to read some words and you're just not aware of it."

Out of the blue, a gigantic headache pounded through her temples. Here she was, trying to nurture a lonely little boy, and now she obligated herself to help Fannie learn to read. Normally that would've been a problem, except... except Elaina wanted... she needed to think about how she could get home--no little problem by any means.

All the while she and Fannie talked, Elaina struggled to listen for sounds coming from Robbie's bedroom. Darn it all, she didn't hear a thing.

Leaning against the hallway wall, she rubbed at her painful head. What a rollercoaster ride today had been, and it still wasn't over yet.

First thing this morning had been the hunt for a dinner party gown, and that meant rooting through the late Countess' wardrobe. Then came hours upon hours of activities running around with Robbie inside the estate house and outside in the gardens.

Oh how she ached.

Next was her washing and fixing Fannie's hair. Truthfully, she'd felt buoyed up by that bit of fun. Then, of course, it had been her turn to be dressed and fussed over in preparation for the formal dinner.

Then, not to forget the stress of being out of time, out of place with a roomful of nineteenth century aristocrats, some of whom would've rather stomp on her than talk to her.

After that came the dance, the waltz. The Duke, Charles... Charlie?... anyway, he had pulled her too close to him... *inappropriately* close... and that had sent her sensibilities into overload.

Frankly, it still did. Without her wanting to, she was getting fond of him. Part of him, anyway. Not the Mount Vesuvius part.

And now this: Robbie misbehaving because he feared losing another mother figure.

She couldn't stay still; she had to pace. "Oh, I wonder what's going on in there."

"Poor Master Robert," Fannie sniffed.

Elena agreed. Well, to be realistic, there were worse things in the world for the Duke to get upset over. So Robbie acted out and had a temper tantrum. Big deal.

The Duke... Charles... no, Charlie... the name Charlie made him seem more human. Charlie would have to deal with tonight's misbehavior. His son needed a loving mother, and from what she understood, Charlie had been a widower for two years. But here was a conundrum: he was a handsome guy; didn't he have any suitable candidates in mind for his next duchess?

He was a virile man; surely he hadn't lived as a monk all this time.

The door suddenly opened and she caught a dark glimpse of Charlie's head. "Fannie. Come," he ordered.

Then his head disappeared.

The maid squeaked. She cast a worried glance at Elaina, and then opened and closed the door.

Wow. Charlie was like a powder keg of dynamite getting ready to blow. And guess what? It was her turn next to face the dragon.

She couldn't help a giggle from escaping. Charlie the explosive stack of dynamite. Charlie the fire-breathing dragon. Charlie the erupting volcano.

Elaina smiled. Charlie the romantic dancer. There were obviously many sides to the Duke of Wolfeshire. What she didn't know was, which side was she going to be dealing with when she entered Robbie's bedroom?

**\* \* \* \***

As soon as Charles entered his son's bedchamber, he changed his course of action. In truth, he had wanted to solidly whip the boy. Robert's disobedience not only disrupted the household, it disturbed everyone, from the lowest scullery maid to Charles himself. And his guests.

Unconscionable.

As for the attack on the housemaid... Charles had to take a steadying breath. Once again his earlier thought returned to him: *No one took advantage of his servants.* Precisely. And that included servants suffering ill-treatment at the hands of the heir to the dukedom.

As he approached the bed and the sunken figure of his son, Nanny Price blubbered her tears while the housekeeper patted the old woman on the back.

Without looking at Robert, he ordered the women to their beds, and also told Mrs. Riddles to give Fannie tomorrow as a day of rest with which to recover herself.

The women scurried out, as he knew they would. Then he closed the distance to the bed.

The room was dark, with a few lit candles on the fireplace mantel and on the bureau. Robert was sitting up, leaning back against his pillow and huddled with the fringed white bedspread around him. His small face was besmirched with tears but he kept quiet and still. Only his clear blue eyes moved, tracking Charles' movements.

That the boy was not crying surprised Charles.

It was then he realized he had made the right decision to discard the idea of whipping as punishment. His own father had whipped Charles as a child many times; as yet he had not exacted the same punishment on Robert. Tonight was not the night to use that form of discipline.

The concern for his son on Elaina's sweet face returned to Charles. *"You... You'll go easy on him, won't you?"* she had asked. The woman had met Robert only two days ago, in spite of the shortness of their acquaintance, she seemed to know him better than the boy's father.

Charles sat at the foot of the bed. "What do you have to say for yourself, Robert?"

The boy rubbed at one eye. "I woke up and... and I was scared."

"How could you be scared? You know you are perfectly safe at Wolfeshire Park."

Robert shrugged his scrawny shoulders. "No, not that way. I woke up wanting Elle. I looked for her, but she wasn't in her room. I forgot she was downstairs."

Robert moved closer to stare at Charles. "She's mine, Father. Not yours. I found her. She needs to be with me. She fears being alone. She's not alone with me."

Charles steepled his fingers as he tried to think of something to say to his son. He knew Elaina had a fear of being alone. Doyle had mentioned that. She had mentioned that.

"Why is Miss Wattell so important to you, Robert?"

"I found her. I helped her. She's mine." He sniffed, and then wiped his nose on the sleeve of his nightshirt.

Charles reached into his pocket and removed a handkerchief. He handed it to Robert.

The boy blew his nose and then handed the handkerchief back.

"You keep it." Charles smiled. "So, it is my understanding that Miss Wattell does not intend to stay here at the Park, Robert. Her home is someplace else. Someplace a great distance away."

"I know! Like the Antipodes! She told me wherever she's going, it's so faraway, the year is different. I'll make her stay, though. She'll stay if I want her to." Robert folded his arms across his meager chest. "Besides, if she leaves here, I'm gonna go with her."

Charles raised his eyebrows. "The year is different? Impossible. How can that be?"

Robert vigorously shook his head. "I dunno, but she said an herb had something to do with it. T-h-y-m-e. Just like time. T-i-m-e. So I told her about the village's healer. That woman uses herbs and potions, too, you know? Like magic. Maybe she can help Elle, and then Elle will take me with her."

Obviously, that was not going to happen.

Charles needed to use logic on the boy. Something to make Robert think about things other than his emotional needs. "What about me, Son? I will miss you if you go someplace else. Indeed, I will be inconsolable."

The boy sucked in his lower lip, obviously considering Charles' words. His eyebrows lowered, but then raised.

"I know, Father! You can come with us!"

Out of the mouths of babes.

Charles ruffled his son's curly hair. "Not so easily done, Robert. Not for me and not for you." He got off the bed and then straightened the points on his waistcoat.

"This is what I will do. I shall have a long talk with Miss Wattell. Tomorrow. Perhaps with some inducements, she might decide to permanently become your governess."

"Good-O!" Robert bounced on the mattress.

"However, Son, your unacceptable behavior must stop. You were given another chance after this..." Charles held up a lock of his now shortened hair. "... and you promised then to be a good boy. As that did not happen, there will not be another chance after tonight, Robert. You are my son, of a great noble lineage. I am depending on you."

The boy lowered his head. "Yes, sir," he mumbled. "I understand."

"Good. I will hold you to that, Robert." Charles turned toward the door. "Now, two things. You need to apologize to the housemaid, Fannie. Tell her a new uniform will be ordered for her and that tomorrow she is not to work. All day."

"Yes, sir. She will like that news."

"Indeed, she will. And then after that, we will have Miss Wattell come in and you will apologize to her for cutting short her time at the dinner party."

"Elle will not be bothered about that, Father," Robert said confidently.

Charles could not dispute his son's words, so he gave his own opinion on the matter. "I care about that, Robert. Miss Wattell was most pleasant to dance with."

Amidst the child's giggles, Charles opened the door and called for the housemaid.

**\* \* \* \***

Now that Fannie had left, it was Elaina's turn. It was with more than a little trepidation that she entered Robbie's bedroom. Despite the few lit candles, darkness enshrouded the area. She could only make out murky forms floating in the shadows.

Fortunately the whiteness of the bedspread provided a bit of a beacon to show her the way.

She spotted Charlie's tall form. "You wanted to see me, sir?"

Then she gazed from father to son. Robbie looked so very small, huddled under the covers as he was. As far as she could tell, the boy appeared no worse for wear.

Perhaps Charlie knew what she was thinking because he cleared his throat. "As you can see, as you requested, I have gone easy on my son, Miss Wattell. The boy has given me his promise to behave, and I have accepted it. He also knows this is his last chance. I will tolerate no additional instances of misconduct."

She stepped forward and took the child's hand. "That's good. I'm glad, Robbie. Being naughty is for little boys, not someone as big as you."

"Precisely." Charlie's voice cut through the darkness. "Now, Robert has something he would like to say to you."

The boy first yawned, and then squeezed her hand. "I sorry, Elle. I sorry you had to leave the party. My father said he liked dancing with you."

Charlie cleared his throat again. Could it be that he was discomforted by what his son blurted out? Elaina bit her lip to keep from smiling. After all, it wasn't every day she saw a duke get embarrassed!

She let go of Robbie's warm hand. "Never mind that. I know all this greatly distresses your father, so I'm very glad this won't happen again."

The boy glanced from her to his father and then back to her. "Will you read t'me, Elle?"

From the corner of her eye she caught Charlie giving a slight shake to his head.

Right. "No, Robbie, you had your nighttime ritual already. And frankly, I'm ready for bed myself. Also, just so there's no mistake, because of tonight's bad behavior, we won't be going swimming tomorrow."

Robbie's lower lip hung out in a pout. "Well, all right. But maybe we can go another day, Elle?"

"Maybe."

She reached over to tuck him in, and then gave him a kiss on the forehead. "Good-night, sweetie."

"G'night, Elle." He closed his eyes and then went completely out.

Charlie then leaned over and patted his son on the shoulder. When he lifted up, he was too close to Elaina and they bumped into each other.

"My apologies," he murmured. Then he took her arm and headed for the adjoining door to the governess' room. He stopped right by it. "You seem to be a sterner disciplinarian than I am, Miss Wattell."

This far away from the burning candles, his features were hard to make out, but she knew, instinctively, that he was steadily regarding her.

The short hairs on her arms stood at attention and she took a step back from him. "We can hope he honors his promises," she whispered. "Now, as I told you earlier, it's been quite a day. I'm looking forward to closing my eyes and having a terrific night's sleep. If you would, please give my regrets to your guests."

She made a small curtsy, and then put her hand on the doorknob.

He moved closer and also lowered his voice. "Elaina, we need to have a long talk. This is something I wished we could have done before. I have many questions."

That he used her name made her smile. "All right. Sure, we'll talk tomorrow."

Stepping over the threshold, she then stopped when he followed her.

"Oh no." She held up her hands, to halt his progress. "We had a deal, *Your Grace*. I go to your party and you never come into this room."

"Elaina, we need to talk."

"That we do, but not right now and certainly not here. So, either you go or... or I'll wake up Robbie so he can be my gallant."

One corner of his mouth lifted as if in amusement. "If I recall correctly, you stated to Lord Nome that you did not need a gallant."

"At the time, I didn't. But now, the master of this house is reneging on his agreement."

"Elaina." He huffed out a breath.

"Charlie," she returned, knowing full well he didn't care for that nickname.

"Hmmn." He picked up one of her side curls and twirled it around his finger. After a couple of twirls, he dropped the lock of hair.

"So, tomorrow then, Elaina. After church services, in my Library. At eleven? Doyle will serve breakfast again."

She hid a yawn behind her hand. "Sorry. Okay, hopefully I'll be awake by then."

"I shall have your lady's maid wake you up in a timely manner." Then he made a bow. "Sweet dreams, Elaina. Have a restful sleep."

He closed the door, and then she was alone. Fortunately, a few candles had been lit so she could find her way to her wardrobe closet. She couldn't help but smile. Tomorrow she had a date with a duke!

# Chapter Ten

The time rang in at a quarter before eleven. It was still morning, and yet a great deal had already happened.

Charles left his double pedestal desk and wandered to one of the Library's windows. Bright sunlight flooded the room. Leaning against the window frame, he gazed out at the frontage of Wolfeshire Park. In the distance, he spied a lone horse--a bronzed gelding--and rider leaving through the Park's ornate gates.

Lord Otto Blankton was in a devil of a hurry, and at that thought, Charles smiled. Earlier, at church services, Lord Otto had continued his courting of the fair Miss Prudence Sinclair. The elder Sinclairs then invited Otto to linger in East Sussex at their neighboring estate for a few days, most likely to ensure that the suit blossomed to fruition.

Charles was happy for his friend. Not only did Miss Sinclair have a substantial dowry, she was quite lovely in features and in disposition. Blankton would be a lucky man to win the lady's heart.

With Blankton's defection from the single state, only four would remain to the Wolfe Pack.

An inconsequential circumstance, to be sure. He had to be realistic. All his friends numbered at least thirty to their years. At this stage in life, marriage and children were high on an aristocratic gentleman's list.

Charles sat back behind his desk. What about his own situation? He had been a widower these past two years. His wife, poor Georgia, had been a vain young woman. Although counseled by the doctor not to use a particular white face powder as a cosmetic, Georgia had ignored the advice. She enjoyed the lightening effect on her skin and was acclaimed to be one of the most beautiful women in England.

However, with beauty came a price. The white particles of enamel or face paint were laced with poisonous lead. Over time, not only did Georgia lose her glowing complexion, she also appeared ten years older along with having her smile ruined by cracked, darkened teeth. In the end, she suffered a paralysis on one side of her face, and shortly after that, she died.

Although the room was not chilly, he shuddered. Shuddered with remembered pain.

However, Robert needed a mother. His troublesome behavior bellowed out that fact. The dowager duchess had always berated Charles for not immediately procuring a suitable duchess to take Georgia's place.

For two years, Charles had not gone along with his mother's wishes. Now, however, it was time. The Little Season in London Society was coming up in a month or two. During the Little Season, he would search the crème de la crème on the marriage mart and select an appropriate wife for a duke.

He sighed. It was a task he was not looking forward to. Marriage to a stranger, once again. However now the stakes were a trifle different, especially now that desirable Elaina resided under his roof.

He was attracted to her; he could admit that, but only to himself.

A knock sounded on the Library door. Charles glanced at his desk clock; the time was wanting only ten minutes to the hour. Was Elaina early? Was she eager to speak with him?

That thought please him greatly. He adjusted his cravat. "Enter."

Instead of the enticing Elaina, the slightly portly figure of Jules Greensby lumbered in.

The man made an expert bow and then shouted, "Wolfe! Here you are. May I have a word with you?"

Charles waved him in. "Of course, Greensby. Sit. What can I do for you?"

His friend sat at the edge of the leather bench across from the desk. He was fashionably dressed, as was usual, however an air of distraction seemed to cover his youthful face and pudgy cheeks.

After taking a deep breath, Greensby lifted his watery blue-eyed gaze and focused on Charles. "It's like this, Wolfe. I can't eat, I can't sleep. I've been driven to distraction by last night's beauty."

Quickly sitting back in his chair, Charles stared at his friend. Greensby was referring to Elaina. He had to be talking about her.

A sick feeling plummeted within him. Charles took a deep breath and held it. He must... he *had* to shake off this awful feeling.

He steadied his voice. "Who are you talking about, Greensby?"

His friend fiddled with one of the brass buttons on his tailcoat. "I come to you, asking your permission. It's my hope you'll give your approval... since the lady whose hand I seek resides in your household."

The devil! Charles got to his feet, to then pace from the fireplace to the opposite wall, and then back again. Any minute now, Elaina would be entering the Library. And when she did, this jackanapes would be pressing his suit.

No.

Fisting his hands so tightly that his fingernails bit into the palms of his hands, he then cleared his throat. "Your acquaintance with this young woman is slight, Greensby. Is it wise to consider her as a partner for life?"

Greensby swiped at his forehead with a handkerchief. "One just knows. Cold logic doesn't rule the heart, Wolfe, but hot emotion does. I took one look at her fair countenance, and I was lost."

Charles nodded. Unfortunately, he understood.

"So, you wish to... pay your addresses to...?"

Lord, Charles could not even say her name.

"I am on tenterhooks. I can only hope Miss Fannie will make me a contented man."

"Miss Fannie?" Charles blinked. "My housemaid?"

"Yes. As soon as she burst into the Blue Velvet Drawing Room last night like one of the avenging Furies, my heart was immediately captured." Greensby then stood and joined him at the fireplace. "I beg of you, man, please do not frown on this suit."

A relief the size of the great Atlantic Ocean filled Charles through and through. "Why, no! I do not frown at all." He slapped his friend on the back. "Indeed, Greensby, I look forward to wishing you and... Miss Fannie... happy."

Thank the good Lord above!

A knock sounded at the door. Charles checked the time. Eleven o'clock sharp.

"Enter," he called out with much relief.

Looking like a ray of sunshine, Elaina stepped in, holding Robert's hand. She wore another one of his wife's gowns--a soft cotton day dress the color of pearl grey with short puffed sleeves and lace frills at the neck. The hem was decorated with satin ribbon bands that also lengthened the gown for Elaina's taller height.

For a moment, Charles drank in her beauty.

"Oh! Hello, Your Grace, Mr. Greensby. I hope we're not interrupting anything?"

"Not at all," Charles assured her. "Come join us. Robert, have a seat on the bench. Doyle will be here shortly with breakfast."

"Good-O! I am as hungry as an elephant! Or a giant lizard!" Giggling, Robert settled himself at the end of the leather bench.

Charles then turned to Elaina. She looked well rested from her night's sleep. Her face appeared dewy fresh and her figure...

He gulped down desire. Yes, her figure was very enticing indeed.

Steadying himself once again, he spoke, "Miss Wattell, Mr. Greensby here has an errand for you, if you would be so kind. He wishes to confer with... young Fannie, to pay his... address to her. Perhaps you can see your way to helping Miss Fannie prepare?"

"*Mademoiselle* Elaina, I would be forever in your debt. Miss Fannie is an angel." Greensby clapped his chubby hands together. "An absolute angel!"

Elaina's delicious mouth dropped open, so surprised was she by Greensby's declaration. For a moment, Charles imagined kissing that mouth.

Her smile brightened the entire room. "Oh yes. Certainly. I'll be delighted to help Fannie prepare." She darted her gaze at Greensby. "Mr. Greensby, I'm very happy for you."

She turned to go, but Charles could not help touching the smooth skin below her sleeve. "If you would please be so kind as to also inform Fannie that Mr. Greensby desires to take a turn about the gardens with her. Assure her that she is quite allowed to do this. She has my blessing."

Her unusual eyes widened, and then she stepped away and curtsied. "I'll let Fannie know."

The feel of her warm skin tingled on Charles' fingertips. He ran his thumb across the tops of his fingers to savor the sensation.

He inclined his head. "Mr. Greensby will wait for her in the Front Anteroom, while Robert and I will be waiting for your return right here, Miss Wattell."

Her gaze darted from him to Robert. "Of course. I'll be back soon."

With a swish of skirts, she was gone. After she left, Charles sat behind his desk again. He was well pleased. A good day's work, to be sure. On this Sunday morning, soon to be afternoon, his Wolfe Pack was now down to three, including him. After the mandatory Sunday lunch of the finest roast beef in East Sussex, perhaps more of the Pack would defect.

In any event, come tomorrow morning, the number would definitely be further reduced. To one. To Charles Burnley.

Once that was done, he would have all the time he needed to decide what he should do concerning the very agreeable Elaina Wattell.

**\* \* \* \***

"By the good Lord above! I am in such a fair pucker! Mr. Greensby wants t'see me? Me?" Fannie almost screeched. "Wot do I wear? Wot do I do?"

In her cramped bedroom, Fannie twirled around like an energetic top.

Elaina had to smile. This girl was in a fair pucker indeed! "First, Fannie, you have to calm down."

"Yes, yes, of course you must calm down, Fannie. You cannot behave inappropriately." Trudy tsk-tsked in her own inimitable way.

It really was a good thing that Elaina had asked Trudy to join her in giving the news to Fannie. The poor kid was about to rocket out into space with her excitement!

Fannie's brown eyes shone like gold, advertising her enthusiasm. She removed a dark green, three-quarter length sleeved gown from her chest of drawers. A frill of lace around the scooped bodice lightened the somber dress.

"Here be my best gown. I know 'tis a little heavy for summer wear. Should I wear this?" Her shapeless eyebrows knitted over the bridge of her small nose.

"This will work out fine." Trudy assured the girl. "I will roll the sleeves up so they'll be above your elbows. That and with the curve of your bodice, you will be able to enjoy any cool breezes that come your way."

Elaina tapped her chin as she looked at Fannie. "While Trudy fixes your gown, I'll work on your hair. Yes, twisted up into a chignon with a curl or two cascading down. That'll be perfect!"

"But I need t'wear my mob cap." Fannie protested. "That'll cover--"

"No, you don't. You're a woman being courted, Fannie. Not a housemaid today."

And maybe, not a housemaid ever again!

It didn't take long to spruce up this darling girl with her gown and with her hair. She didn't have a mirror in her bedroom, but Trudy had fetched a handheld one so Fannie could admire her new appearance.

"Look at me! Look at me!" Fannie crowed. "I love how my hair curls and shines. I look like a lady of quality, don't I?" She rustled the skirts of her gown back and forth. "Thank you! Thank you both so much."

Both Elaina and Trudy smiled at this demure young woman. Chances were very good that after today, her fortunes would drastically change for the better.

"So," Elaina clapped her hands. "Let's get you downstairs to the Front Anteroom where Mr. Greensby is waiting to take you on a turn about the gardens. So romantic!"

"And I shall be your chaperon," Trudy made a slight curtsy. "Following at a discreet distance, of course!"

The three of them left Fannie's bedroom feeling very happy indeed. That Mr. Greensby was so enamored of dear Fannie? Priceless!

Once Elaina formally introduced the pair of would-be lovers, she then waved goodbye and headed for the Library. She couldn't wait to eat breakfast, and to see Robbie and Charlie again.

**\* \* \* \***

As soon as Elaina returned to the Library, Robbie greeted her.

"I saved some breakfast for you, Elle. I wanted to eat it all, but Father told me it wouldn't be polite."

She had to bite back her smile. "No, indeed. I thank you for... um, curbing your appetite." Smoothing down the skirt of her grey-colored muslin gown, she sat by Robbie's side.

Then she looked over at her host. "And I thank you as well for pulling the reins in on this boy otherwise I'd have to go hungry until lunch or dinner."

Charlie's lips twitched. "I am certain Mrs. Parson's kitchen can produce additional breakfast items should you desire more food, Elaina."

Ooh. Just the way he said her name made her innards tingle with delight.

She dimpled a smile. "This cornucopia of eggs and toast will be fine for me, thank you."

Seeing Robbie's woebegone eyes as she picked up her fork, she took pity and handed him a piece of bacon, which he promptly chomped down on.

Funny how seeing Charlie so... so darn appealing as he sat behind his desk actually put her hunger on hold.

Instead of eating, she took a sip of tea. "So, Charlie, are we ready to have that talk that you were so urgently wanting to have last night?"

"Charlie!" Robbie giggled. "Can I call you Charlie, too?"

"No, Robert," Charlie admonished. His gaze then focused on her. "Elaina, do you delight in vexing me?"

"Most definitely!" She nibbled on a piece of toast. "Vexing you is the highlight of my day."

He pressed his firm lips together, not in annoyance, but to prevent himself from smiling. She was absolutely sure of that as if he'd told her so.

Then he toyed with the center bow on his cravat. "After you have had your fill, I thought we could also go for a long walk in the gardens... and beyond if you like. The weather is very fine. Too fine to remain indoors."

"And there we'll have a talk?" She wanted to clear the air with him. She *needed* to clear the air.

"Precisely."

She took two more bites of toast and then was done. "So, okay, let's have our walk. Maybe we'll run into Mr. Greensby and Fannie."

Charlie waited for her to stand, and then he did, too. "I emphatically hope not. Greensby is smelling of April and May too heavily for the sensibilities."

She had to laugh. "How can you say that with a straight face?"

Robbie indulged himself with a fit of the giggles. "Ho, Father! How can you say that with a straight face?"

Huffing an exasperated breath, Charlie urged his son from the Library. He then placed his hand on her back to lead her forward, but inadvertently slipped his fingers under the tasseled cord that decorated her high-waisted gown.

At least she thought it was inadvertent.

A tug pulled her back and she glanced at him.

"My apologies, Elaina.

He didn't look apologetic.

"Hmmn," she commented.

As they headed for a back door to the gardens, they passed Alastair Dover, Lord Nome, coming from the upstairs.

"Well, well, well," he said with a smirk on his handsome face. "Don't you all look like a family."

Elaina frowned. The man didn't mean those words as a compliment. In fact, she sensed some hostility. Or envy. How very strange.

While Charlie talked with Lord Nome, hopefully for just a moment, she and Robbie walked out into the dazzling array of sunlight, the fresh fields of daisies, and the warm summer air.

Robbie handed her a straw bonnet that had been hanging on a post by the back door.

She arranged it on her head and tied the ribbons under her neck. "It's so beautiful here, Robbie. And peaceful. You're a very lucky boy."

"I dunno. Maybe. But I'm lucky I found you, Elle." He gave her a cheesy smile and then ran down a path circling the flowers.

Elaina shielded her eyes from the sunlight to look for him. The bonnet's brim helped, but too bad she hadn't grabbed her sunglasses.

Robbie came dashing back, almost hopping with excitement. "Guess what? Guess what? Edgars wants my help in pruning a beech tree. He says it was split by lightening and now he has to fix it."

If she remembered correctly, Edgars was Wolfeshire Park's head gardener.

"May I? Do you mind, Elle? I like to watch Edgars snip and trim tree branches. Rather like what you do with your scissors, right?"

"You're right. Pruning and haircutting are rather similar, aren't they? Sure, Robbie. I think it would be fine with your father."

She heard a heavy step behind her. "What would I be fine with?"

It was Charlie, of course, and yet it wasn't. He had a scowl on his face as if... as if Mount Vesuvius was about to explode again.

Yikes. Even though the day was super sunny, Charles Burnley, the Duke of Wolfeshire, blew as cold and as stormy as a devastating hurricane.

*Blast that Nome. Blast him to hell.*

Charles strode out from the main house with murder on his mind. Murder against Alastair Dover. Charles wanted to crush that devil's very soul. It had been very difficult indeed not to plant a facer on Nome's smug face.

What Nome had said; what he had insinuated... Damn it all. It did not bear thinking about.

However, what that man had warned... well, Charles could not fault the man for speaking the truth. Cavorting about with a female who had unknown antecedents would only bring shame upon the House of Wolfeshire. Elaina was not only not of his class, the differences in their stations were astronomical. Her birth was far below Charles'. Even establishing her as a mistress would dilute not only Charles' reputation, but Robert's as well once he became of age, exposing them both to endless ridicule from the Bon Ton.

And the fact that she had come to Nome, offering her body in exchange for his protection...

Unconscionable!

Charles' blood roiled and burned within him. He felt... betrayed.

He had to distance himself from that woman--now. Quickly. As soon as possible. And Robert had to, as well. It was unfortunate that his son was so taken by her, but nonetheless, the woman had to go.

There was no doubt in Charles' mind now: Elaina Wattell *had* to leave Wolfeshire Park.

Reaching her position, he thrust a lightweight spencer at her. "Wear this," he said tightlipped. "While you are here, you are expected to act like a lady."

He ignored her raised eyebrows and astonished expression.

Dismissing Robert to the head gardener's care, Charles waited until his son scurried off.

In the interim, Elaina slipped into the jacket. "What's this all about?" she asked.

"I am the one who will be asking questions, something I regret I was remiss in when you illicitly arrived here at the Park."

He spotted a wooden bench in the shade of a cluster of European Beech trees. An expanse of daisies surrounded the bench. It was a very pleasing setting, however, he was in no mood to be pleased.

"We will sit here," he proclaimed, and sat first on the bench, and why not? After all, this woman was no lady.

She gracefully took a seat at the other end of the bench. Her gaze contained reproach, but that mattered not a whit to him. She was an impertinent jade, and the sooner she left these premises, the better off they all would be.

He folded his arms across his chest. "Now, tell me again where you are from and how you arrived here."

Her nostrils flared, but she kept her temper in check by settling her hands in her lap. "As I told you, I'm from the United States, from the city of New York. The last thing I remember was that a friend of mine tried hypnosis on me in the hopes of curing me of a childhood fear."

Her voice picked up as she became more animated. "When you go into a trance, everything seems to slow down, you seem to be removed from everything, set apart. It's as if the world keeps going, but you're not in it anymore. There's a type of decreased awareness of the physical world. When I woke up or came out of the trance, I wasn't there with my friend, I was here in your Park, with Robbie tugging on the hem of my blouse."

She told him nothing new. Drumming his fingers on his folded arms, he waited for her to continue. Although it almost physically hurt to look at this impertinent piece, he forced himself to.

"I've been thinking about this--a lot," she added. "I mean how could I be on one continent and then wake up across the Atlantic in a different..."

She stopped.

Whatever she was going to say was important. "A different what?" he prompted.

Pressing her tempting but traitorous lips together, she shook her head, refusing to answer. Then she said, "No. I think the change in locations is enough to talk about."

He shrugged. Her words were not important. "How do you intend to return to your home?"

She sighed. "Well, that's the problem, isn't it? But actually, your son gave me an idea."

"Robert? What the devil have you--"

"Calm yourself. I did nothing." She reached down and pulled up a white-petal daisy. "I just asked him what he would do if he found himself in similar circumstances. He mentioned that there's a healer in the village who uses herbs. One herb, thyme, was growing around the tree where I went into the trance. I'm thinking that maybe this healer might be able to duplicate what happened to me and help me get back to where I came from. It's a long shot, but it's all I have."

He almost snorted. "You delude yourself if you believe magical herbs can propel you to another land."

She plucked a petal from the daisy. "Well, if it doesn't work, I'll just have to think of something else."

"Something else like asking for a man's protection?" He glared at her.

"I believe I asked for permission to stay here only until I could sort things out. That is all."

Removing his top hat, he ran his hand through his hair. Then he settled the hat back on his head. "You need to leave. You staying here is not good for my son."

If he was not mistaken, he saw her eyes widen. He heard her huff a breath. Then after a moment, her expression steadied. "So my time here has run out. That's right, isn't it? That's what you're saying?"

She kept plucking daisy petals.

Devil take it! If only she kicked up a fuss or actually cursed at him, he would have known how to deal with her. As it was, she just sat there, placid. Her behavior made him question his actions.

But why should he question his actions? She was a nobody. She had no right to the opulence of Wolfeshire Park. She had to go. His ancestral estate was not going to be further sullied by this loose woman with her loose behavior. Especially since he had wanted to... he had looked forward to...

No. He was a proud man with a distinguished heritage. The Wolfeshire name had to be protected.

He could not keep still so he got to his feet and paced in front of her. "This is what I will do, Miss Wattell. I will provide a carriage to take you to London."

*Out of sight; out of mind.* That was the ongoing refrain in his head.

Her dainty mouth dropped. "Now?"

He took in the sight of her plump lips and then hardened his heart further. He lifted a judgmental eyebrow.

"Okay, I understand. You want me to be gone now." She pressed those tender lips together. "So, instead of London, I'd like a lift to the village healer."

He pointed his index finger at her in an imperious fashion. "I want you away from East Sussex. The village is not far enough by half."

"Fine!" She pulled the last petal from the daisy. Then she let the stem flutter to the ground. "Honestly, I don't know why you're being this way... I had thought... Never mind. It's fine."

Standing, she lifted her nose. "I'll pack my things and be on my way. By the way, thanks for letting me stay here three nights. That was very civil of you, I'm sure, especially since... well, you don't think much of me."

She started back toward the house.

He grabbed her around her upper arm. "Complaining to Robert will not change my mind."

She glared at him until he released her arm. "I have no intention of complaining to your son. If you would, please give him my regrets."

She then continued her way back to the house.

This woman made him so angry. He felt like roaring out his displeasure. He had been happy with her. He had pictured her and him growing closer... until they shared the same bed. But what did she do? She propositioned Alastair Dover right under Charles' nose.

Something niggled at him. Something did not make sense. Why had she chosen Nome to proposition, and not Charles himself? After all, *he* was a duke.

Watching her gentle sway as she calmly returned to the back door to the house, he yelled after her. "The carriage will be at the front entrance in thirty minutes. Be there."

She did not turn around, but only lifted her arm as acknowledgement that she had heard.

He narrowed his gaze. His hands itched to strangle the woman.

How dare she... how dare she...

Walking back over to the bench, he picked up the discarded daisy stem and twirled it around. It reminded him of something; a game. A game the French played where one person pulled petals seeking to divine whether the object of their affections returned the regard. *"He loves me, he loves me not."*

Had that been what Elaina was doing? What had been the answer: a yea or a nay?

The devil!

Hurrying over to the stables, Charles arranged for his tilbury carriage to be readied. This carriage traveled well on rough roads. Elaina could not grumble that she had received an inadequate ride to London.

At the appointed time, the tilbury waited out front, as did Charles. He needed to make certain himself that she was bundled up and off his estate.

Thirty minutes came and went. Enraged, he ordered his servants to produce the woman. After searching every level and every room in the house, the servants reported back empty-handed. She was nowhere to be found in the grand house.

Charles had gotten his wish, however it was not quite the way he had envisioned it: true, Elaina Wattell was gone from Wolfeshire Park, but not on his terms.

He frowned. Where, on God's green Earth, was she?

# Chapter Eleven

Tramping about in the wilderness wasn't Elaina's idea of a good time however, as the old saying went, *"desperate times call for desperate measures."*

Yep, she was desperate all right. Desperate and heartbroken.

Thick-trunked gnarled trees with a bounty of endless leaves made traveling difficult for one as city-bred as her. She wasn't too nervous about her primitive surroundings. Not yet, anyway. And she didn't mind when tree branches inadvertently brushed her face or caught on her clothes. But soon, in a few hours, night would fall and she'd be alone, in the dark, at the mercy of whatever feral animals happened to wander her way. Or hear her tentative steps. Or smell her deep-seated fear.

*Don't think about that. You'll be okay. Just focus on going in the right direction.*

She *hoped* she headed in the right direction--to the nearby village and of course, the herbal healer. Earlier, maybe yesterday, she'd asked Mr. Doyle about the village. If she headed in the correct direction, she'd arrive at the village center in an hour. However, that was by horse or carriage. On foot, it would take longer, of course.

*Keep going. Keep going. You can do this.*

Maybe. She was a realist. Maybe she could do this. If not then... she shrugged. At least she hadn't gone along with what Charlie wanted.

Her heart constricted. What had happened? She might've been overly optimistic but she and he, they seemed to have a connection between them. Not that she expected romance or anything like that, but honestly, they could've been friends, and they both cared for Robbie.

But, geez! Charlie came out of the house wanting to pulverize her into dust. So, the only explanation was that something or someone in the house had poisoned his mind against her as quickly as a flash of lightening. And that person had to have been, most likely, Alastair Dover, Lord Nome. Why he would do this... who knew?

That was as far as she could go with her supposition.

She heard the trill of a bird and some rustling noises coming from the ground debris. Nothing to be scared of... yet. She had to keep plodding ahead, following the direction of the setting sun.

Truthfully, she didn't envy Charlie when Robbie found out she had gone. The dear boy wouldn't react well--to put it mildly--and he wouldn't mince any words about how he felt about her departure. Or rather, on her being kicked off the estate. As she herself had heard, the boy had a set of lungs, and he wasn't afraid to use them.

A hoot of an owl startled her. Okay, enough conjecture. She had to keep focused.

Wearing her twenty-first century blue jeans and top, along with a handkerchief scarf and a short buttoned jacket--courtesy of Robbie-- she hoped to be taken for a boy or a man. She'd wound her hair up in a coil and kept it hidden under a military type of forage cap--also Robbie's. Of course the zipper on her jeans was in plain sight so she wore a small linen apron that she'd picked up from the kitchen.

She carried a beat-up leather satchel that contained a few gowns altered for her use, and that was all. As for the clothes, she didn't think Charlie would care one way or the other about her taking some of his wife's things.

Then again, she hadn't thought he would've tossed her out like yesterday's trash, either.

Oh well. Not only yesterday's trash, but yesterday's news. Putting those depressing thoughts behind her, she picked up her pace, trying to make good time.

**✳ ✳ ✳ ✳**

Charles feverishly paced in his Library. Then he stopped by the window to look out at the dying sunlight. The setting sun reminded him he was running out of time. Soon the night would be upon them.

He ran his hand over his shortened hair. As soon as it was confirmed that Elaina was no longer on his estate, he knew he had made a mistake. A monumental mistake. A tragic mistake. No matter what her character, she was a woman alone. A very vulnerable woman with no assets other than the obvious ones. The sensuous ones she had attempted to lure Nome with.

However... that did not make any sense. If she had offered her body to Nome, why would he have refused her? After all, his deadly sin was lust. If Nome had wanted her, which of course he did, he would have taken her. He had no scruples about stealing one of Charles' domestics. Not like Greensby, who addressed his feelings to Charles and then had asked permission to court the housemaid Fannie.

Charles felt his blood run cold. He had assumed his friend was a man of honor... perhaps though, he was not. Charles had listened to the devil, and now he was suffering in hell.

Robert burst into the Library. His brilliant blue eyes were narrowed with sparks of hate. "You made her go away. Why? She wasn't yours. She's mine. I found her!"

"Robert, I--"

"No! I hate you! You lied. You said you were gonna make her stay. She was gonna stay here with me forever." The boy sank down on the leather bench and set his chin in his hands. "I will never forgive you."

Charles sat next to his son. He tried to place his hand on the boy's shoulder, but was rebuffed.

"No. Don't. D'you know what it's like to get tucked into bed? To have a goodnight kiss? To know you have a best friend in all the world?" The boy blinked watery eyes at him.

Charles had to sigh. "In truth, Robert, no. No, I do not have those experiences."

"Well, I did. And now she's gone." The boy jumped up and went to the window. "Out there, somewhere. D'you know she's afraid of being alone in the woods? She's really, really afraid. I helped her. I protected her. I made her safe." He shivered. "She must be... so terrified now."

Charles stood. He could feel it; he could feel her panic. His decision made, he rushed to the Library door. "Come. I must assemble teams to search for her. I will find her, Son. I *must* find her."

As soon as he and Robert entered the Front Anteroom, the butler hurried over. His flushed face appeared even ruddier than usual.

"Your Grace." Doyle made a bow. "There has been no news. How may I help?"

Charles nodded. "Have a team wait at the village healer's cottage. I feel certain that is where Miss Wattell is headed. In the meantime, every available man is assigned to this hunt." He paused. "Not Lord Nome. That man is no longer welcomed in my house. I wish him gone."

"Yes, sir. Very good, sir. I shall ensure that this is taken care of." Doyle inclined his head.

Grabbing his huntcap as if this was a foxhunt, Charles then turned to the butler. "We shall use the foxhounds to track Miss Wattell. All of the dogs. We can cover a much larger area that way."

"I'll get one of Elle's dresses," Robert piped up. "The hounds can use that for her scent."

"Good lad! Excellent idea." Charles ruffled his son's curly hair.

While Robert raced upstairs to the governess' bedchamber, Charles hastened out to the stables. The dogs would track Elaina; soon they would pick up her scent. Once that was done, it would not be long before they found her.

With any good luck, it would be before nightfall.

Charles closed his eyes to say a silent prayer. He had wronged her; he had wronged her terribly. He did not know what he could do to make up for this egregious error but whatever she wanted, he would do. He would try to make things right for her no matter what it took.

**✳ ✳ ✳ ✳**

The setting sun looked so pretty beaming its rays of fading light through the dark leaves of the forest. It was kind of like a lightshow. Elaina had an excellent seat and didn't have to pay a dime!

Yep, it was a perfect spot to rest for the night. She huddled in between the cracked curves on the trunk of a greenwood tree and gazed up at the darkening sky.

She wasn't scared; not yet anyway. She had warm memories of Robbie insisting that he was her protector. That she didn't have to worry about being alone because he had saved her.

Maybe he was right. Maybe she could finally put her childhood trauma behind her. After all, she wasn't two years old anymore. She'd gotten rescued from the ravine all those years ago, and also had gotten rescued--by Robbie--with her unexpected trip to the nineteenth century. Now, all she had to do was stay still and calm, and hopefully by the morning, she could continue her journey to the village.

Good.

A cool breeze filtered through the leafy trees. She didn't have a blanket to wrap herself up in but she did have a few long gowns. They'd serve double duty for tonight.

After tucking herself in, she used the leather satchel as a pillow and then with a sigh, she closed her eyes. All in all, she was pretty darn comfortable.

Sure, she hurt thinking about how Charlie had scraped her off the bottom of his boot. Maybe she'd made more of their connection than there actually was. Honestly, it was his loss, not hers.

Who needed a duke, anyway?

She stuck her tongue out at him and then settled in for a hopefully uneventful sleep.

The scent from a once-worn garment was not as vivid as from a living organism however Charles felt assured his hounds would pick up Elaina's scent. He divided his teams into eight, to cover the vast acreage of Wolfeshire Park. Each team was followed by four dogs.

The night sky was nearly fully black. He and his four hounds made their way into a forest of greenwood trees; the dogs would sniff, get excited, and then grow quiet again. Every time that happened, his spirits rose. And then, of course, they would sink. He wanted to be the one who found Elaina; however that was not the important issue. That she was found was what mattered. That she was found and had suffered no mishap.

Suddenly, he saw all four dogs move cautiously and then they stopped and wagged their tails. They did not bark, which was unusual.

Dismounting from his steed, he tethered his horse to a nearby tree. He grew anxious to see what the hounds had discovered. There was enough light for him to make out a lump on the ground. It was a reclining figure draped in... in female clothing.

May God be praised!

He threw the dogs a goodly amount of treats. They had done extremely well. By all that was holy, it was Elaina laying there, covered by dresses and with a forage cap hiding her long hair.

He got to his knees and then smoothed his fingers over her soft cheek. Thank the Lord she was safe. Thank the good Lord above.

"Oh!" She quickly sat up and stared at him. "Who are you? Why are you here?"

"It is me, Elaina. Charles. I have come to apologize and take you back to the house where you belong."

"Oh no." She pushed his hands away from her. "I'm not going back with you."

The hounds had finished their treats and now lumbered over to her to be petted and praised for their good work. A few even indulged in giving her a lick.

"Good dogs." She patted them down. "Sorry you had to be put to work on this fine Sunday evening."

He took her hand and held it between his own. "Elaina, I know what I did was unconscionable. I also know that it is too soon for you to forgive me. I hope you eventually *will* forgive me. May I say Robert is anxiously waiting for your return, as are a great many of the servants."

His voice wavered. "I-I know I do not deserve your kind regard, but... I vow I will do whatever you wish. I will try to make things right no matter how long it takes."

"Wow, that certainly is a change of heart." With her other hand, she pulled off her cap and released her cavalcade of hair. "Why do you feel differently now? I'm still the same person I was this morning. Same birth, same no-status class, same mysterious vaulting over the continents."

He could not help himself; he had to reach over and feel her silky hair. Lovely. He twirled a strand around his finger. "To my shame, I unfortunately listened to a blackguard. I should have known he was not to be trusted. As I said, I do hope that in time you will find it in your heart to forgive me."

"Hmmn." She pushed away his hand and started folding up her dresses. "I bet it was that Lord Nome fellow. He's too handsome for his own good."

Charles lifted his eyebrow. "You believe Nome is handsome?"

She shrugged. "Sure. As in he thinks he's God's gift to women type of handsome."

"Perhaps you are right." Charles took the folded gowns and filled the satchel. "He is a scoundrel. He said... you, er, you offered yourself to him."

"What?" She actually snorted. "As if that would ever happen. Yuck."

Yuck, indeed! Charles held out his hand for her to take. "I am chastised before you, Elaina. Come. Please allow me to take you home."

She placed her hand in his, and as God was his witness, he suddenly felt whole. As if she and he were meant to be.

Standing, Elaina brushed off her very strange apparel. Trousers made of an odd material, an apron, a boy's jacket... and her feet... her toes showed through the leather straps on the shoes.

The apron was loose on her slim hips so he reached over and removed it. Now revealed was an interesting type of enclosure on her trousers starting from her waist and down onto her lower belly. The trouser material buckled, revealing something metallic.

Intrigued, he reached over to touch the shiny fastener. "What is this, Elaina?"

She violently swatted his hand away. "None of your business."

She was right, of course. He had no business touching her so intimately.

In truth, he was a chastened man. "Will you allow me to take you home? Please, Elaina?"

She huffed a breath. "Well, okay. "You know, 'home' sounds good. Very good. I really am tired. And I can't wait to see Robbie again."

"I shall take care of you, my dear. I promise."

Charles helped her onto his horse, and then mounted behind her. The scent of her hair, the feel of her rounded bottom settled in against him; in this intimate position, every muscle in his body tightened at this unexpected pleasure.

He cleared his throat. "My son is beside himself to see you again, too. Elaina, you... you have made a difference in both our lives. Now, rest against me and I will have you home in no time at all."

At first unyielding against him, she then allowed herself to relax.

He tightened his hold on her. Lifting the reins, he urged his steed forward. As well trained as always, the hounds followed. With his arms now wrapped around his treasured prize, he carefully made his way through the greenwood forest.

# Chapter Twelve

*My, how things have changed!*

Elaina sat like a queen in her bedroom, eating a delicious breakfast with Robbie at the room's small, two-chaired table. Yesterday she'd been kicked off the estate. Today, Monday, August twenty-first, she was reinstated as governess to the heir to the Duke of Wolfeshire.

A new day and a new phase in her life back here in 1820. But... But what should her next step be?

On one hand, she felt a tremendous pull to seek out the village healer and hear what the woman had to say about Elaina's bizarre situation.

On the other hand, she longed to explore this "new" relationship with Charlie. He had been so contrite last night, so remorseful for his actions. As he should've been, of course. He even seemed to be appreciative to have her in his life. What that meant in the long term though, she didn't know, but just thinking about him made her heart pound out an enthusiastic beat.

Should she forgive him? Maybe. Maybe not. The jury was still out. She'd see how he acted, how he treated her. She'd see if he genuinely cared for her or if all he cared about was stations of birth: bluebloods versus redbloods.

She lifted her nose. She could be snooty too!

As for Robbie. Goodness, the boy had been so excited to see her last night, he almost cried. And she almost cried. Goodness, they were such a pair!

Sitting across from her, Robbie smeared apricot marmalade on his slice of toast and then crunched into the bread. "I'm glad we ate in your room, Elle. I didn't want to go downstairs. I don't want to share you with anyone."

She dimpled a smile at him. So sweet! "Ever, Robbie?"

"I dunno." He shrugged his slender shoulders. "Right now I don't want to let you out of my sight. Maybe, I dunno, three years from now?"

"Ah! I see. So you're my jailer?" Of course she was kidding.

"What?" His brilliant eyes bugged wide. "No! Elle, I just want--"

"Relax. I'm teasing you, Robbie."

He left his seat to come over to her. Then he curled his arms around her and laid his head on her breasts. "I never want you to go. I love you, Elle."

She kissed the top of his head. "I'm honored, sweetie. I love you, too."

That realization burst inside her. She *did* love this child. In such a short space of time, she loved him. He needed her and she needed him just as much.

There was a knock at the door, and Trudy entered holding a slew of fancy boxes. "Now, now, Master Robert. No inappropriate behavior allowed."

Robbie lifted his head to stare at her. "What do you mean? I'm just hugging my Elle."

"And your Elaina has to get dressed. Sitting around in your robe, *Mademoiselle* Elaina, is frowned upon. And, inappropriate in the company of the opposite sex." She tsked-tsked.

Elaina sat, speechless. "Are you serious? Robbie is only seven!"

Robbie stood facing Trudy, with his back to Elaina as if protecting her. "I'll save your reputation, Elle. I'll marry you. Don't worry. I'll take care of you."

She had to giggle. "That's very kind of you, sir, but completely unnecessary. So, now that we have that out of the way, Trudy is right. It's time for me to get dressed. What are those boxes?"

Trudy shooed the boy back into his own bedroom. "'Tis your new wardrobe, straight from London. His Grace's valet, Wilkins, has just arrived with all these boxes in tow. Allow me to assist you in dressing."

Elaina gazed at the mountain of boxes now on her bed. "Wow. Are you sure these things aren't to be divided among all the women at Wolfeshire Park?"

Trudy's serious face lit up with a smile. "You are a jokester, that's for certain, Elaina."

After the smile, it was all business. Elaina hurried over to the bed to see what treasures Charlie's valet had brought her.

**\* \* \* \***

Holding Robbie's small hand, Elaina made her way down the marble steps of the grand staircase. She wore one of her new gowns; this one was made of light blue grey sprigged muslin. The décolletage was a bit low for her comfort, but with grey satin ribbon trim and puffed short sleeves, she felt very confident that she was dressed... well, appropriately!

The hour was nearly eleven, and once again she and Robbie were headed for the Library. She wanted to discuss with Charlie the possibility of hiring a tutor for his son, and also, if she were truthful with herself, she wanted to see if he still felt the same way as he had last night.

Of course there was still the matter of going to see the village healer, but frankly, right now she was concentrating on what was here, not what was back for her in the twenty-first century.

Robbie barged right into the Library without first tapping on the door. "Father! Father! I'm to marry my Elle!"

Oh good gosh! Her mouth must've dropped straight to the floor!

Charlie, sitting behind his desk, gazed from his son to her without batting an eye. "Indeed? So I am to welcome Elaina as a new daughter-in-law?"

Mr. Doyle, who was standing in front of the desk, covered his mouth with his large hand, probably trying to hide his amusement.

Elaina knew she was flushing as brightly as a ripe tomato. "No, no. Robbie is just..." Just what? "Just making a joke," she finished.

"I'm not, Elle." Robbie led her over to the leather bench to sit, and then he sat next to her. "I was in her bedchamber this morning and she only had on a robe. Trundle was scandalized."

Mr. Doyle obviously couldn't help himself. He coughed into his hand."

Charlie's lips twitched. "I see you are a very fortunate young man.

However, there is no need to call for the parson, as yet."

Since Charlie took the "happy" news in stride, Elaina settled back against the cushion on the bench. He wasn't concerned; so she wasn't concerned. Most likely Robbie would soon focus on another topic.

The butler bowed. "I shall go inform Nanny Price on her new circumstances. As for the other situation you entrusted to me, His Lordship assures me he shall depart this afternoon."

"Good." Charlie waved his hand. "The man is *persona non grata*."

Lord Nome, evidently.

After Doyle left, Robbie scooted closer to Elaina. What's the circumstance with Nanny Price, Father?"

Charlie picked up a book, a ledger, and flipped it open. As he glanced at one of the pages, she admired the curve of his strong jaw, the brush of his sideburns, and the twist of a curl falling down onto his forehead. His cravat was precisely tied, his navy tailcoat buttoned, and the sleeves of his white shirt peeped out from the edges of his tailcoat sleeves.

Her heart gave an extra beat of approval.

His desk chair squeaked as he leaned back in it. "A picturesque cottage has become available on the grounds of the Park. I have reserved it for your nanny, Robert. Your former nanny. It is time the dear woman retired and looked to her own concerns."

Elaina had to ask. "But how will she live?"

He inclined his head at her. "She shall be well taken care of. She will still be a member of this household however, she will not be responsible for this hellion."

He pointed a stern finger at Robbie.

From the floor where Robbie now played with a puzzle, he looked up and giggled. "I'm a hellion!"

"Not exactly something to boast about, boy." Charlie pressed his lips together.

She patted Robbie's head to show that his father wasn't to be taken seriously on this matter... she hoped anyway.

"So." She folded her hands in her lap. "That's sort of what I wanted to talk with you about today."

"And what is that, Elaina?" Charlie unflattened his lips and smiled at her.

She fidgeted with her fingers. "Well, after what happened yesterday, I feel like we really need to clear the air. Between you and me, I mean. Also, as you know, I'm not really a governess. And obviously I don't know about your current affairs, and things like that. I'm thinking Robbie needs a dedicated tutor."

"My current affairs?" Charlie lifted his eyebrow. "I don't have a current affair, Elaina."

She made a face. "Ha ha. Very funny. You know what I mean. Now that the war with France is over, what's next? Robbie needs to be learning foreign languages, geography, you know, substantial subjects. He's a very bright boy. He needs intellectual stimulation."

Charlie's lips curved to the side. "Indeed, we all need stimulation."

She felt the burn of heat on her cheeks. Was the man flirting with her? Honestly, it had been so long since she indulged in flirtatious behavior, she'd almost forgotten how to go about it.

He sent her a cool glance. "Not to worry, I shall take your suggestion under advisement. I do value your opinion, Elaina." Then he cleared his throat. "Please allow me to say you look particularly dashing in your fashionable morning gown."

She smoothed the material on her thigh. "A whole ton of boxes just got delivered this morning with this dress included. Thank you so much! I can't possibly wear all of the clothes; there are so many. You're very generous."

"Not at all." He smiled again. "I am extremely thankful you are giving me another chance."

Robbie snapped a puzzle piece in place. "Father got himself in a bumble broth, that's what the servants say."

"Bumble broth?" She tilted her head at Charlie.

"A bit of a mess, my dear. And yes, indeed, I did. And please allow me to say I am very thankful that you are here now with us."

For a long moment, she and he regarded each other. Goodness, she violently tingled as if she'd stuck her hand in an electrical socket. She stared at his wonderfully thick lips. What would it be like to kiss him?

A noise intruded. The butler hurriedly entered the Library and stood in front of the desk.

"Your Grace!" Mr. Doyle bowed. "I am sorry to interrupt, however Lord Martiz suddenly collapsed. He has fallen, and seems to be in agony. He cannot tolerate being moved. Shall I send for the doctor?"

Charlie abruptly stood. "Yes, at once. Where is Lord Martiz?"

"He is in the Main Hall, sir. His Lordship had his bags packed and was on his way out when he sank to the floor."

First helping Elaina to her feet, Charlie then gestured for Robbie to stay and finish his puzzle. "Come, Elaina. Martiz suffers from an old war injury to the head. Perhaps we can ease his mind until the doctor arrives."

Elaina quickly followed Charlie. Maybe she could somehow help Lord Martiz.

The poor man was writhing on the Italian marble floor in the Main Hall. The anguished sounds of his pain must've carried through the great house. Goodness, it hurt to even look at the man in his misery.

Elaina ran over to the injured lord and sat on her knees by his side. "Lord Martiz, I'm Elaina Wattell. We met Saturday night. Can you tell me what's troubling you?"

His hair, a wispy russet color flew this way and that as he thrashed his head about on the floor, moaning and groaning with every turn.

"Old war wound, milady," he muttered. "Those damn Frenchies blasted bloody holes in my skull." He touched the area by the curve of his right ear and also in the corner of his right eye. "Hurts like the Devil's cock."

"Oh." The words took her aback but she supposed it was an apt description.

She felt a hand on her shoulder and looked up into Charlie's dark eyes. "Martiz also suffers from inappropriate speech. Another souvenir from the gunshots. Before his service, he was the mildest of men."

Poor fellow. She smoothed hair off of the man's forehead. "Lord Martiz, the doctor is being sent for to attend you, but it's going to be a little while before he gets here. Would you like for me to massage your head while we wait?"

Charlie squeezed her shoulder. "Are you certain this is a good idea, Elaina?"

"Why not? It might give him some relief."

Lord Martiz fluttered his eyelids. "Yes, please, milady. Drive this fucking pain out of my head."

Oh gosh. This man was in agony.

"Martiz, please," Charlie grimaced. "There are ladies present."

"It's okay, Charlie." She then asked the horizontal man, "Can you sit up, Lord Martiz? Can you stand?"

"No. No! The pain..." He kept his eyes closed.

Hmmn. She needed clear access to his entire skull. Scooting on the floor, she sat cross-legged by his head and then lifted his upper body onto her lap. Now she could get her hands on his head.

Charlie squatted down beside her. "Elaina, that is a... a rather intimate position. I cannot allow you to subject yourself--"

"He needs help." Turning her face, she spoke into Charlie's ear. Wow. He sure smelled good. "Let me help him, Charlie. It's just a little massage."

"All right, Elaina. I support you."

She started with lightly massaging all over Lord Martiz's head. It must've helped for his moaning quieted but his shoulders still shifted about on her lap. Next, she focused on one of the areas he had pointed to: behind the curve of his right ear. This area in phrenology was known as the Animal area, specifically, combativeness. Using her fingertips, she gently pressed on the spot, circling her fingers up and down, massaging and rubbing.

Lord Martiz let out a moan, but it was a soft one. It didn't sound painful.

The last area she massaged was by the man's right eye. This was the Perceptives area, specifically, language. Once again he made a sound, but it was more of a sigh.

His breathing deepened and his heavy head lolled to the right on her breast. He slipped into a deep sleep.

"You astonish me, Elaina." Sitting next to her, Charlie's warm breath tickled her cheek.

And that warm breath sent urgent messages deep into her core. Mmm!

Then he pulled away and snapped his fingers for the butler. "Doyle, see that Lord Martiz is placed back in his bedchamber. As soon as the doctor arrives, send him up to the room. With any good luck, perhaps the doctor is unnecessary. Perhaps Elaina has already restored Martiz to working order."

After two robust footmen carried the sleeping lord from the Main Hall, Charles stood and then leaned over to lift Elaina to her feet. For a moment they stood close, close enough for her to inhale his masculine fragrance.

More mmm. She couldn't help her actions; she leaned in closer to him.

Then a clapping sound echoed into the large area.

The very handsome, but hugely egotistical, Lord Nome stepped into the hallway. "By Gad," he shouted. "The woman wags her tail at all of us. She flaunts her fine body at me, then holds Martiz in her succulent lap, and now she throws out lures to a duke."

He clapped again. "Well done, madam. Well done."

Elaina had hardly time to blink. She saw Charlie, with fisted hands, rushing over to Lord Nome. With a practiced swing, he knocked the man flat on the floor.

Lord Nome was out--cold.

# Chapter Thirteen

Charles flexed his hand. His knuckles hurt like the very devil, but blast, the pain was worth it!

Snapping his fingers again, but wincing with a bit of discomfort, he called over his butler. "Doyle, please dispose of this annoyance."

"Yes, Your Grace. With pleasure, Your Grace." Doyle then uncharacteristically grinned.

While the butler arranged for two additional footmen to remove the reprehensible... and down-for-the-count Earl from the Main Hall, Elaina moved and stood by Charles' side.

She placed her hand on his lower arm. "Charlie, you punched him out for me."

"Did I?" He tried to hold back a smile. "I believed I was ridding Wolfeshire Park of a bothersome pest."

Then he placed his hand over hers and squeezed it. Lord, she felt... she felt like magic.

Another voice was heard, coming from the opposite direction of the hallway.

"I saw it! You planted a facer on the blackguard!" Robert came running and enveloped Charles in a hug. "Father! You tapped the Earl's claret!"

Charles' smile threatened to break free. He cleared his throat. "I did not draw blood, Robert. The man insulted our Elaina. I could not let that stand."

"No, indeed," Robert agreed. "I'll punch him out, too." He swung his fist.

"Gentlemen." Elaina put her arm through Charles', and also took Robert's hand. "I thank you both, but let's move on with our day, okay? That man ruined yesterday for us; I really don't want to think he spoiled today as well."

Charles patted her hand. "A very fine idea. Let us take a stroll about the gardens and have that talk that we intended to have yesterday."

Elaina nodded. "And then maybe we can visit the village healer. I need to know... I *really* need to know if she has any ideas on how I can get home."

Charles glanced at his son but fortunately the little fellow had not been paying attention. By all that was holy, Charles *did not* want Elaina to return to her home--wherever that was. Her place was here, with him and Robert.

He recalled his son's earlier words:

*"D'you know what it's like to get tucked into bed?*

*To have a goodnight kiss?*

*To know you have a best friend in all the world?"*

Those were three things that Charles *would* like to have. That he *would* like to experience... with Elaina, and only with beautiful Elaina.

Walking outside into the lush summer heat, he absentmindedly played with her slim fingers as they curved around the crook of his arm. He needed to use all his persuasive abilities to convince her that no matter what the village healer had to say, Elaina needed to stay here at Wolfeshire Park with both Burnleys. That *they* were her destiny, not anything on the other side of the Atlantic.

Charles wanted her; he wanted her more than anything. The big question here was: what was he going to do about it?

Mindful of yesterday afternoon's debacle, Elaina grabbed a straw bonnet and a spencer before stepping outside. Now sitting on a bench in the field of daisies, she glanced out at the cheerful array of flowers. Daisies, specifically ox-eyed daisies, were such a familiar sight to her. Usually, they were considered as unwanted weeds, but here, blooming in their own environment, the colors of the pure white petals centered by lemony yellow seemed to burst onto the senses like a joyful exaltation of flowers.

She had to sigh. So much had happened in such a short period of time. Had it only been four days since she mesmerized her way back into the past?

Charlie sat beside her, close enough for their thighs to touch. He smiled over at her. "Robert has been pressed into service by my head gardener. Evidently a few rosebushes inadvertently got chopped down by the junior staff. Edgars feels he can save the bushes."

The chill of a breeze filtered through her so she leaned against Charlie to steal some of his warmth. "Robbie is a fantastic little boy. Who knows? Maybe one of these days he'll be known as the Gardening Duke."

Charlie curved his arm around her shoulders, pulling her even closer. "Elaina, I have a question to ask."

For some reason her stomach jumped. What was on his mind? Did he... did he want to know why she didn't quite fit into this time period?

She shook that thought off. "Sure. What is it?"

He reached down and pulled up a daisy. "When you plucked the petals from that daisy yesterday, were you playing the French divination game? You know the one, *'He loves me, he loves me not.'*"

Wow. He remembered that! The heat of embarrassment burned her cheeks. "Actually, yes. Yes, that was what I was doing with the daisy."

He murmured into the shell of her ear. "What was the answer, yea or nay?"

Then he moved away to look at her intently. So intently, she felt as if she was suspended in space, in time, with no past or future. Only the here and now.

She took a deep inhale. "As a matter of fact, the answer was he loves me." Then she wet her lips. "I don't know if it's the truth, though."

With his fingers, he turned her face toward his. "It *is* the truth, Elaina. As impossible as it sounds with our very short acquaintance, I do love you."

Then he trailed his fingertips over her lips. "And I would very much love to kiss you."

"Oh." She stared into his deep chocolaty eyes. Her breathing increased ten-fold. "Oh, yes. Let's--"

He kissed her. A slow nibbling of the lips, the slight pressure to the touch, and oh, suddenly she was yanked into a fantastic world; a world filled with all the senses, maybe even more than five. Her entire body woke up as if it had always been asleep.

She turned so they were closer still. Lifting her arms around his neck, she ran her fingers through his silky hair and slid them up and down and all around his head.

*Mmm.*

He was gentle, as gentle as a first kiss could possibly be, but then he roughly pressed for her open mouth. She eagerly complied.

*Mmm.* A swirl of delight!

His tongue sent shivers of desire pulsing through her. This tangling of tongues urged her to go higher, higher, to insist on more, more.

"Elaina," he murmured against the column of her neck, stopping and kissing the notch at her neck's base. "You are magnificent. All I have ever desired."

"Charlie." No other words could pass her lips. His name said it all; she was totally and completely his.

Well, maybe. Again, the jury was still out.

His lips moved lower, to scorch a path down to her clavicles. He kissed the left collarbone and then the right. For a moment she felt his hot breath on the bulges of her breasts, teasing her, driving her crazy, but he then traveled his lips up to her earlobe, to nibble there.

"Charlie," she moaned. "Oh, I want you!"

He crushed her to him, her breasts flattened, eager for the contact. Then his mouth hungrily covered hers, and quite frankly, she was lost in time, lost in this delicious haze of love and longing.

How much time passed, she didn't know, but when they parted, her lips violently tingled, urging her to continue their lovemaking.

"Elaina." His eyes now darkened to the inky blackness of space. "You are so sweet, like honeyed wine, like... nothing I have ever known."

She missed his warmth. She missed his lips. A shiver ran through her. Goodness, she missed their dreamy intimacy.

He removed his tailcoat and settled it on her shoulders. "It would not do for you to catch a chill. My son and I could not bear to lose you."

Leaning against his strong shoulder, she sighed. "Don't worry. I feel fine. I feel more than fine, actually. You..." She felt herself blush. "You sure know how to kiss."

He threw back his head and laughed. "Kissing you, well, I am certain I could kiss you all day, my dear."

Trailing his fingers up and down her bare neck, he then lifted her hand to kiss her knuckles. "I must confess, I envied my friend with his close position to you, on your lap, his head next to your bosom. I wanted to tear Martiz away so I could take his place."

What could she say? She wanted Charlie's head on her bosom, too!

He then suddenly kissed the tip of her nose. "Come. Let us visit that village healer. It is my fervent hope the woman knows nothing about mesmerism, about traveling great distances in the blink of an eye. In that way you will know. You belong here, with me and with Robert."

Elaina slid her arms into the tailcoat's sleeves. "But if the healer does know what to do?"

"If she does, then it is a decision you must make. I... I am offering myself. I am offering my possessions. I am offering you my heart. What does your home back in the Americas offer you?"

Standing, she then walked with him, back to the house. Honestly, she didn't know the answer to his question. A few days ago, she had thought she was all set in life. Her dream of opening her own salon was on the brink of happening. Of being a reality. She had her mother; she had her friends. She had everything she had ever known. But...

But how could that compare with this? With Charlie? With Robbie?

Charlie still wasn't aware of the time difference between them. Before she made any kind of decision, she had to tell him. She had to let him know just how different she really was.

# Chapter Fourteen

Elaina could admit to being nervous. Sitting in the carriage outside the healer's rundown hut, she glanced at the man by her side. He loved her; she knew he did. She felt safe and secure in his company. And maybe, for the first time in her life, she didn't feel afraid. If she had been standing outside this hut by herself, sure, she would've been nervous but no, not afraid. Robbie had cured her of her fear. And being with Charlie was sweet icing on the cake.

She looked up at him and smiled.

He smiled back. "Are you ready to go in?"

"Yes. Sure. I guess I've been sitting here long enough." Gosh, she sounded excited, didn't she?

He helped her down from the carriage. Robbie had already jumped down and began exploring the surroundings while Charlie tethered their carriage's horse to a flourishing oak tree.

Then Robbie came running over from the back of the hut. "Can I stay out here to play with the dogs, Elle? There are four of them, all mixed in color. They want to fetch sticks."

How could anyone say no to his darling face? "Okay. But don't tease them. And don't wander off."

Charlie stepped by her side. He nibbled on the curve of her ear. "Just the very words I would have said... had my son deigned to ask me."

"Oops! Did I overrule your parental authority?"

"Not in the least, my dear. My son likes to listen to you."

"Enter, enter," came a voice from inside the hut. "I wait for you."

Right. Time to face her demons head on.

Elaina went in first. The hut, obviously a temporary structure that could be put up or taken down at will, was dark inside. Dark and fragrant with herbal smells. Hanging around the walls were bunches of different herbs, but frankly, all she could identify and inhale was the lemon, grass, and lavender scent of thyme.

Standing in the dark was a woman. Young or old, Elaina couldn't tell. She had a large reddish scarf covering her head. Just a smidgeon of her black hair could be seen. She had a heart-shaped face with pinkened lips and large, dark eyes. As for clothes, she wore many layers: a blouse, a vest, a raggedy skirt, an apron, a cape. Her feet were bare.

"You come in. I waiting for you," a woman's gravelly voice said.

Elaina stepped closer. "Hello. I'm Elaina Wattell, and this is Charlie Burnley."

He removed his hat. "I am the Duke of Wolfeshire, ma'am. I have seen the village healer many times before; I do not recognize you."

A flash of a smile brightened the woman's face before it disappeared. "I come for this one, Duke." She pointed at Elaina. "The healer allowed me this time with her. This one has question only I can answer."

Ooh. That sounded spooky. Elaina stepped a little closer to the woman. "I do have a question. I was wondering if you could help me with something."

Suddenly a brilliant light arched through the darkness revealing the shabby interior and also the woman. She was in the full bloom of maturity, with wise eyes and a knowing smile.

With a quick movement, the woman turned down the oil lamp until the light was tolerable, not overly bright.

"You call me Lily." She gestured toward two rickety chairs. "Sit. Tell me your concerns."

Sitting side by side, Elaina couldn't help reaching for Charlie's hand. He clasped her hand in his. So comforting!

*Okay, here goes.*

"Lily, I come from far away. Very far away. A good friend of mine thought she could hypnotize me to overcome a longtime fear of mine. Hypnotism is like mesmerism--a type of trance or sleep. I think it worked at first, but then I passed out and woke up here, on Charlie's lands. I know that sounds impossible, but it did happen." She snapped her fingers. "It happened just like that."

The woman narrowed her eyes and nodded. "Yes. Yes, I see. You make wish, did you not?"

"Well, yes. I..." She looked over at Charlie. "I know this is going to sound strange, but yes, I actually wished for a duke, but--"

"Indeed?" Charlie lowered his eyebrows. "That is most peculiar, Elaina."

"Hear me out. Back there I knew two men--cousins--with the last name of 'Duke.' Either one or both were going to help me with my business, my hair salon. So, I don't know, 'wishing for a duke' just came to me."

"A wish was granted for you, Elaina." Lily bobbed her head. "That and for healing. Your mother Tessa and your friend Leila arrange this 'Thyme', the herb, this Thyme Transference."

"What? What are you talking about? How do you know about my mother?"

"She distressed over what you suffered as a babe. She work and pray to get you whole. She know that friend is part Gypsy. She ask Leila to help."

*"What?"* Elaina vaulted out of the chair. "How do you know this? How can this be?"

"Elaina, why are you alarmed?" Charlie also stood and placed a comforting arm around her.

"Is truth," Lily murmured. "Leila ask for my help. She kin to me."

Oh, good gosh. Elaina held onto her head. It was spinning. She *knew* it was spinning.

She stared at the woman. "You know Leila? But how? She... and me... we're from the future. Over two hundred years in the future."

"Elaina?" A look of pure panic flashed in Charlie's dark eyes.

"It's true, Charlie. I've been wanting to tell you but, honestly, that sounds so incredible, so farfetched, I didn't know if you could believe me."

"It is truth." Lily bobbed her head again. "I confirm. So, why you here, Elaina? You desire to take back wish? You want me to count to three for wake up as Leila would have done? You look to go back to city rat-race?"

Elaina rubbed at her temple. "This is so unbelievable. It's hard to understand. My mother... my friend..."

"They do fine. They know. They happy you are happy." Lily held out her hands, palms up. "Is truth."

It had to be the truth. How else would Lily know about Leila, and her mother Tessa, and the traumatic event when she was very young? What had Leila said? One of her long ago ancestors dabbled in hypnosis...

Wow. It was crazy, insanely unbelievable, but then again so was time-travel.

She turned to Lily. "You've spoken with them? You're saying you're related to my friend Leila?"

"I have visions." The woman shrugged her broad shoulders and then rubbed her midsection. "As for Leila, I carry her great-times-five grandmother now. Indeed, I shall call this one 'Leila.'"

Omigosh! How mind-blowing this all was.

"Your choice, Elaina. Decide your future." Lily said solemnly, as solemnly as a judge.

Elaina sucked in on her lower lip. What was she to do?

Charlie lifted her hand and gently kissed it. "May I say I hope, I fervently hope, you choose me, my dear one? To be with me and Robert for the rest of our lives?"

Deep inside, she knew the answer. She probably had known it all along. After all, she'd also had a wish, when she'd been only two. A wish for someone to find her. To protect her from the darkness of the forest. To be with her forever.

That person was here, standing by her side.

She slipped her arm around him to give him a side hug. "I do. I do choose you, Charlie. What I've been looking for all my life is right here... with you."

He slid his hands up her face to cup her jaw and then he kissed her.

*Mmm.*

"Lovely." Lily pulled down a sprig of thyme and ran it through the air surrounding them. "'Tis done now. My job done. You go."

Elaina broke the delicious kiss and turned toward this magical woman.

"Thank you. Thank you so much. I think... I *know* this is the answer I was looking for. But, Lily, can we do anything for you... and your baby?"

"You kind lady, as I knew you would be. My thanks, but soon I meet my other half. On the road to London, we meet. He not aware of me as yet, but I will convince him to be with me." She winked.

Elaina rushed to give Lily a hug. Charlie inclined his head, and then escorted Elaina outside. But he then turned and went back into the hut. What was he doing? She strained her neck to see what was going on. She saw him handing Lily a large handful of gold coins. Guineas? Sovereigns?

His deep voice carried out to her. "A token of our thanks, Madam Lily. If you are ever in our area again, please stop by and see us. You will be most welcome."

More murmurings, and then Charlie stepped outside.

"Come, love." He held out his arm to encompass her. "We have a great deal to talk about on the return trip back to the Park."

She sighed. "Yes, we do. But what about Robbie? Should I tell him about... you know, coming from the future?"

He helped her into the carriage. "My son will be more interested in the news that you have decided to stay with us." Charlie leaned against the bench cushion. "Do you think I will have to engage in a duel with Robert for the honor of your dainty hand?"

She leaned over and kissed Charlie's forehead. "You're incorrigible! Get Robbie and then we'll go home."

Home. What a wonderful word.

* * * *

Frankly, on the way back, Elaina didn't feel like speaking. The enormity of everything washed over her like a tidal wave, leaving her wits scattered and dashed into bits against the shore. But in a good way. In an overpowering way.

She sat in the middle of the carriage, with Charlie handling the reins and Robbie pressed up next to her. The boy was, in a word, ecstatic.

"Now you'll never leave me, Elle," he insisted.

She nodded. "I never will, sweetie."

At that, Charlie reached over and kissed her hand.

They were almost back at Wolfeshire Park when a beautiful horse with a tall rider passed through the ornate iron gates.

"That stallion is of the finest breed." Robbie stared at the horse. "Arabian, you know. I want one."

So impetuous! She smiled at him. "You can't have everything, Robbie."

He looked up at her. "I don't need everything, Elle. I have you."

Ooh! Her heart just about jumped right out of her chest!

"Out of the mouth of babes," Charlie murmured. Then he glared at the horse's rider. *"Him."*

Lord Nome, obviously.

The man urged his horse in the carriage's direction, so Charlie slowed down his lone horse.

"State your business and go, Nome," he snapped.

Lord Nome bowed his head. "Wolfe, *Mademoiselle* Elaina, and young Robert, I... I need to tender my apologies. My behavior has been dismal."

"Indeed, it has." Charlie pulled up on the reins for a stop. "Now you need to go."

"Wait." Lord Nome held up his hand. "Although it does not excuse my behavior, may I say it was envy that drove me. I saw how you and your son were around *Mademoiselle* Elaina, and I... I wished for the very same type of connection. And if I couldn't obtain it, then I was determined that no one would have it."

He lowered his gaze. "I have been an arrogant arse, forgive me."

"Nome--"

"Please, let me." Elaina interrupted Charlie. "There's been no harm done, Lord Nome. We wish you all the best in finding your own special partner for life."

Lord Nome bowed his head. "You are too kind, *Mademoiselle* Elaina."

"Indeed, she is." Charlie smiled at her and then turned back to Lord Nome. "So, now I say again, Nome: go. Perhaps if I can look beyond your deceit, I might decide to invite you to the wedding."

Nome lifted a dark eyebrow. "I see. Yes, I would very much like to wish you both happy."

With a tug on his top hat, Nome angled his horse back to the road. Charlie then urged his horse forward.

Elaina tapped on his arm. "Didn't you forget to ask me something?"

Robbie nearly did a jig in his seat. "I agree! Elle, I can do a better job of asking you!"

A slight twitch lifted Charlie's lips to the side. "My hand was prematurely forced by that... blackguard. Elaina, would you mind very much if I ask you a very particular question once we arrive at the house and are..." He glanced at his son. "And we are alone?"

Elaina dimpled a smile. "That sounds perfect, Charlie."

# Chapter Fifteen

Entering Wolfeshire Park's Main Hall, Charles had envisioned taking the future Duchess of Wolfeshire into a secluded room, perhaps the Garden Study, to then ply his love with champagne, woo her with kisses, and propose that they join their lives together in holy matrimony.

Alas, this was not to be. To be sure, he *would* propose, however at this very moment, there was a commotion the size of greater London shaking through these halls.

As soon as Robert took off for parts unknown, the comical figure of Jules Greensby suddenly appeared. He pulled on Charles' superfine tailcoat sleeve with little regard for the fact that this jacket had been masterfully created by London tailor George Stultz.

"Wolfe! Wolfe! A thousand pardons but I must impose on your generosity." Greensby must have recovered his senses because he then bowed to greet Elaina. "*Mademoiselle* Elaina."

Charles removed the man's grasping hand. Begad! The man was animated... no longer governed by sloth. There was nothing resembling the trait of idleness about Jules Greensby on this day.

"What is it, Greensby?" Charles impatiently stated. "I have my own agenda I wish to follow today."

The man's chubby face shook with his distress. "I have just returned from London, procuring a special license for Miss Fannie and me to marry. May we conduct the ceremony in your private chapel?"

Elaina clapped her hands. "Oh, that is lovely, Mr. Greensby. I'm so happy for both of you."

Charles could not help grumbling. He wanted his own happiness insured. But for now, he supposed he would have to put that on hold.

Instead, he considered another side of the issue. "Greensby, what is the haste? You are well-known to never make rush decisions."

Greensby worked his mouth until he forced his words out. "A man knows what he knows, Wolfe. And I know I want Miss Fannie for my wife." He pounded on his chest. "I am changed for the better!"

Charles sighed. "Yes, I understand the urge." After a wink at Elaina, he snapped his fingers for the butler. "Doyle, let us see what we can arrange on this short notice. Perhaps the parson can see his way clear to come down to Wolfeshire Park's chapel. We have Lord Martiz still here if he feels up to attending. Greensby, if you wish, I shall act as your witness. Who will be... Miss Fannie's?"

Greensby exchanged a glance with the butler, then spoke, "She has chosen Miss Trundle as her witness."

Elaina lifted up on her toes to whisper into Charles' ear, which gave him a thrill deep into his core.

"How about Mr. Doyle acting as Mr. Greensby's witness instead of you? If I'm not mistaken Trudy and Mr. Doyle really like each other."

"Do they?" Charles lifted an eyebrow at Doyle.

He had no idea his butler and the lady's maid were sweet on each other. Somehow, even though Elaina had been at the Park for such a short time, she had discerned this.

His chest bellowed out with pleasure. She would make an excellent duchess.

"Greensby, instead, Doyle will be your man. He and Trundle will complement your wedding party."

After shaking his friend's hand, Charles glanced at his butler. By the good Lord above, Doyle actually puffed up. Indeed, Elaina was right again!

With that done, he escorted his bride-to-be from the Main Hall. If they were fortunate, the impromptu marriage would most likely begin in an hour or two. And after that... well, then he would concentrate on wooing his own special partner for life: Elaina, soon to be Mrs. Charles Burnley, the Duchess of Wolfeshire.

**\* \* \* \***

The marriage was beautiful. Fannie certainly glowed with happiness. Elaina had styled the young woman's thick hair into an upward twist with short ringlets hanging down from the top, at the base of her neck, and surrounding both sides of her small face. Her sienna brown hair shone with a glimmer that was distinctly reddish thanks to a bottle of henna dye Elaina had found in the Dowager's things.

Fannie's hair was gorgeous! There would be no mob cap for this young bride!

At the back of the chapel, Mr. and Mrs. Greensby stood, hand in hand, receiving well wishes from the guests. On such short notice, the guests were mostly the staff at the Park. Nanny Price was present, as was Lord Martiz. He exclaimed to all and sundry how thankful he was for Elaina's ministrations. He even said that he now felt as good as he had before Bonaparte's blasted war.

Oddly enough, Lord Martiz blushed when he had said, "blasted." Evidently he had no need to use inappropriate words anymore.

During the ceremony, Charlie had been a bit antsy. He waited until the marriage had been solemnized by the parson and a toast proclaimed. Then he insisted on spiriting Elaina away from the festivities to a room she hadn't seen before: the Garden Study.

It was a tranquil room, set a distance away from the hubbub of the front entrance. On a low table in front of a Thomas Chippendale gilded settee, stood a bottle of French champagne along with two fine crystal goblets.

Charlie helped her to the settee cushions. "It is past time we concentrate on ourselves, my dear." He sat beside her. "Robert even insisted I 'come up to scratch', although where he heard that vulgar phrase, I will never know."

"He's the sweetest boy." She had to giggle. "I can't help but feel that everything is going to fall right into place for him and for us."

Charlie poured the champagne and handed her a glass. *"Now* it is time for us. It is our time." He clinked his glass with hers. "To the future."

"But what about what I told you, Charlie? About me being from *your* future."

"You *are* my future, Elaina. I do not deal with abstractions, only with the here and now. I do not care about unusual circumstances. I shall paraphrase my friend Jules Greensby: *A man knows what he knows. And I know I want you for my wife.*"

Charlie stole a kiss. "Hmmn, good," he proclaimed, and then he stole another one. "I love you, Elaina. I cannot imagine my life without you. You bring joy to this house. Love and wisdom, as well. Every member of Wolfeshire Park is for the better, knowing that you are here, and will be its mistress."

As he spoke, she remained quiet. Her gaze took in his shortened haircut, the line of his sideburns, his dark as midnight eyes, the slight hollow of his cheeks, and his penetrating chin. When he lifted her hand, she enjoyed the feel of his skin against hers. He was warm, strong, and knowledgeable.

Honestly, she was just so happy, all she could do was soak everything in.

He kissed her fingers. "Here is the formal part of my proposal. Where I 'come up to scratch.' Would you do me the honor of becoming my wife? To stay with me always? To mother my motherless son?"

Charles kissed his way up her hand to her elbow. "To tuck me into bed? Give me a kiss or two at night? Be my best friend in all the world?"

She threw her hands around him, the force of which pushed him down on the couch. "Oh, Charlie! Yes! Of course I say yes. You are... Omigosh, what can I say? I wished for you, Charlie. I wished for you to be my duke. I do love you."

Even though the couch was not overly wide, he maneuvered to be on top, hugging and kissing her to her heart... and her body's delight.

Elaina couldn't help sighing with all that she was. Here was her life's true joy. With Charlie, she knew she would never be alone again.

# Epilogue
## One Year Later

Today was Elaina's first wedding anniversary. One year ago on August thirtieth, she and Charlie said their vows in the private chapel at Wolfeshire Park. Eleven months later, they welcomed Tessa Anastasia Burnley, born on July nineteenth, the day George IV was crowned at his coronation ceremony.

Obviously Charlie had missed George IV's lavish spectacle. Not that he minded one bit. He was so proud of his new baby girl; Charlie almost was impossible to live with! Besides, he wouldn't have enjoyed seeing Queen Caroline denied admittance to the grand affair in London. Then again, at least in Elaina's view, Caroline had never acted as a queen for the British people.

It was too bad, however, that Caroline died just three weeks later.

But life goes on. Carrying her six-week-old, Elaina carefully took the grand staircase down to the Garden Study. It was such a tranquil room, with a fantastic view of one of Wolfeshire Park's flower gardens. She had fond memories of this room; this was where Charlie had proposed. This was where they'd first made love.

Laying the baby in a wooden cradle, she hand-rocked Tessa to sleep.

She waited for Charlie to return from his friend's wedding. Viscount Martiz--Kenneth--married a young lady to the North, in York. Now that Lord Martiz was no longer troubled by headaches, he'd been eager to find his own partner for life.

Elaina was very happy for Lord Martiz.

Also, Lord Otto Blankton wed Miss Prudence Sinclair a week after Elaina and Charlie had tied the knot. Now that Lord Blankton no longer had to worry about money--to a degree anyway,--he allowed himself to enjoy more of what life had to offer. Prudence was his happy helpmate. Last Elaina had heard, the Blanktons were on the lookout for a suitable match for sister Constance.

As for Fannie and Jules Greensby, they were the proud parents of a bouncing baby boy, one week older than Tessa. They often stopped by Wolfeshire Park to visit, not only Elaina and Charlie, but also married couple George Doyle and wife Trudy, who both continued to serve at Charlie's estate.

The only member left of the Wolfe Pack was Lord Nome. He was still decidedly single. Some would say Nome was enjoying his bachelorhood by sowing his royal oats, as it were. Elaina would've said he couldn't hold onto a woman... after all who would want him? He didn't know the first thing about being loyal or considerate. The man was obviously flawed and had no desire to change.

His loss.

Warm sunlight flooded the Garden Study and Elaina's position on the settee. She felt so relaxed, so content. Closing her eyes, she allowed her mind to drift on these delicious sensations. She felt her heart rhythmically beating. Slow, slower, slowest. Then, a type of low buzzing traveled through her... it was a beckoning hum that seemed to open a portal into... into someplace else.

Absolutely magical.

Then, she saw a vision of her mother Tessa, and her friend Leila. They smiled and waved at her, obviously happy for this connection. They looked so good. Elaina missed them. A moment later, they disappeared and the figure of healer Lily, took their place. She held up a baby girl close to Tessa's age. After Lily smiled, her image also disappeared.

Something tugged on Elaina's sleeve, bringing her out of this trance.

"Elle! Elle! Father just got back. He has presents for us. Even for Tessa. For me, he brought a whole set of soldiers. Now I can beat Napoleon Bonaparte!" Robbie's brilliant blue eyes almost glowed with his excitement.

He was now eight years old... and almost an exact copy of his father, except for those hauntingly blue eyes.

"That's wonderful, Robbie." Elaina gave him a kiss on the cheek.

Of course, finally, Napoleon Bonaparte was no longer a worry to be feared. On the fifth of May, he died in exile on the island of St. Helena's.

She heard Charlie's deep voice coming from beyond the Garden Study. He was probably making his way to this room. Her heart beat faster. She'd only have to wait to see him just a little while longer.

"So, what did your father get for the baby, Robbie?"

"A rattle! So she can make noise. Here it is." Robbie pulled a sterling silver rattle from his pocket and shook it so the three bells on it jingled.

The rattle had the large face of a court jester. Maybe the face was a bit scary but Tessa probably would enjoy hearing the bells.

"I love it! I'll have to thank your father."

"You have to thank me for what?" Charlie suddenly stepped inside the room.

"Charlie!" She ran over and threw her arms around him, feeling his solid chest. "Oh, I've missed you!"

"And I you, dear one." For a moment, they lost themselves in a delicious kiss.

*Mmm!*

Robbie pulled them apart.

Charlie ruffled the boy's hair. "I have been gone nearly two weeks, boy. I have killed people for less."

Robbie wrinkled up his face. "Oh, go ahead. Kiss Elle. I just won't look."

Sitting down by the cradle, Robbie placed some of his new soldiers around it. Playtime!

Hugging Elaina to him, Charlie murmured into her ear, "I shall take Robert up on his generous offer."

And so he did.

More *mmm!*

After a time, he kissed the tip of her nose, and then looked down into the cradle. "And how is my darling little Tessa?"

"She sleeps, she eats, she cries... in addition to getting diaper changes. You know, she takes care of business." Elaina gazed at their daughter's little round head covered with dark wispy curls. "And she laughs, too, and loves to smile. She's a love."

"Like her mother." He kissed Elaina again. "I am the happiest man on this good Earth."

"And I'm the happiest boy," Robbie chimed in. "What did you get Elle, Father?"

"What did I get your mother?" Charlie looked over at the door and gestured to Doyle.

The butler brought in something large, about the width of her outstretched arms. A painting, perhaps? Whatever it was, it was covered with paper.

Charlie took the package and set the bottom edge of it on a table. "Happy anniversary, darling."

"Ooh, thank you! I'm intrigued, Charlie. What in the world is it?"

He lifted his eyebrow. "Take a look."

"Okay." Carefully tearing at the paper, she turned the canvas around and saw a beautifully vibrant rendition of a field of daisies--white petaled daisies.

Curving his arm around her waist, he pulled her into him. "These daisies have the correct number of petals so that if you 'pick' them, you will always know I love you."

Her eyes flooded with tears. "That is so beautiful! I love it! I love you!"

She kissed Charlie until, honestly, her toes curled and her heart sang!

Robbie shook his head and looked over at his sister. "They're at it again, so keep your eyes closed."

Of course Tessa was still sleeping so her eyes remained closed.

Robbie turned back to his soldiers. His Elle had gotten her wish for a duke, but he'd gotten his wish as well: his wish for a happy family with Elle, and also now with Tessa.

Good-O!

# The End

# If You Enjoyed This Book

If you enjoyed reading WISHING FOR A DUKE, I would be honored if you gave this novel a review. Your input is valuable to me! By leaving a review you help other readers come across new works, and that, in turn, helps me.

Thanks again! :))

Happy Reading!

*Susanne Marie Knight*

# An Excerpt From:
# AN UNUSUAL MASQUERADE

A Time-Travel Regency Romance

Read on for an excerpt of Susanne Marie Knight's 5 star Time-Travel Regency Romance, AN UNUSUAL MASQUERADE.

*An ancient time mechanism is accidentally activated,*

*sending modern-day Helene back to 1813.*

Available now at Amazon.com.

# Prologue

Eversham Hall, Southwold, Suffolk, England

1813

Sebastian D'Brooke, the Duke of Eversham was lonely. Heartbreakingly so. However, the cause of his loneliness could be laid at his own particular door, no one else's. At the advanced age of three and fifty, he never married, nor formed an alliance, or was that a *misalliance?,* with any of the young ladies he had selected over the years to warm his ducal bed.

No. No wife, no mistress, no children, and obviously, no grandchildren. No blood relations to take over the reins of the dukedom when Sebastian passed, except for that blockhead cousin, Miles Fredricks, Esquire.

A dilemma, that. Or perhaps his lack of a connection could be considered a tragedy.

Naturally, over the years he pondered this problem. He vacillated over one solution, then another, without ever choosing an outcome. There had always seemed to be time to make a decision.

Time. Time had been his lifelong passion. Everything, even the matter of an heir, took second place to his obsession with the concept of time.

Walking to the open window in his workshop bungalow, Sebastian glanced out at manicured frontage and pebbled pathways leading to his grand estate, Eversham Hall. It was a known fact that the Hall was the finest in Suffolk, England. Perhaps in all of England.

All was quiet outside; no visitors or busy servants scurried about to disturb his solitude. That was the way he liked it; that was why he spent most of the day at his secluded workshop, away from the main Hall. The only noise he could hear was the ticking and tocking from the many pendulum clocks spaced out along the walls in the bungalow.

Sebastian loved clocks. He loved all kinds of devices that told time: mantel clocks, ormolu clocks, watches, sundials, hourglasses, in fact, anything used to measure time. Timepieces were his passion. He could even say in all honesty that the clocks kept him company. He considered himself not an *amateur* horologist--a person who dealt with timekeeping apparatuses--but a *professional* one.

And now, today, Tuesday, the sixth of July in this the year of our Lord 1813, he was almost finished with his *pièce de résistance*.

Returning to his crowded work area, Sebastian sat in a wooden chair and adjusted his spectacles. Strewn out on the tabletop were the intricate bronze gears he had created for the ultimate device in dealing with time. A mechanism that actually accessed time in the past and also time in the future.

Seemingly impossible, and yet...

He brushed back the white fringe of hair constantly falling into his eyes. Truth be told, he had not come up with this idea on his own. Years ago he had been an adventurous sort. He had often gone diving in the waters of the North Sea, near his estate. One fortunate day, he had come across the remains of an ancient Roman vessel. Amidst the wreckage of rotting lumber, he discovered the fragmented pieces of a small device. A device constructed of bronze with numerous precision-made gears and dials commonly found in timepieces from eras past.

The purpose of this device had puzzled him ever since.

Until now.

Finally, after countless hours... countless years of translating the Greek inscriptions on the device, he deciphered the meaning and function of the object. He deconstructed it and then made dozens of missing parts. Lastly, he fashioned a replica to, hopefully, duplicate its function.

As it turned out, this mechanism was based on time. And now he was almost ready to begin his scientific experiment.

His plan was this: take a seemly routine voyage around the British Isles on his personal schooner, *Tempus Fugit,* Times Flies. Obviously, since that blasted war with the French--with Bonaparte in particular--was still raging on, the sailing would be confined to English waters. Then when the ship reached an energy grid line that was required for activation, he would set the mechanism in motion.

To be truthful, Sebastian was not certain of the outcome. Would his schooner be thrust back into the past? Or instead would the *Tempus Fugit* be vaulted into the future?

Perhaps there would be some other reaction entirely. Something he had not anticipated. It was possible. Anything was possible.

A knock sounded on the door. His long-suffering butler, Dobbins, entered the congested workshop holding an elaborate tray filled with refreshments.

With his pinched nose, bulbous chin, and dark uniform coat and jerkin, Dobbins was a somber sight. The man nasally intoned, "It is time for tea, Your Grace."

The butler glanced around the overcrowded spaces, and, hard-pressed to find an empty spot for the tray, sighed. "I shall obtain another table, Your Grace."

"No, no, I will make room." Sebastian stood, and then swept aside loose papers and stray tools, which then allowed Dobbins to set the tray down.

While the butler prepared his tea in the preferred manner, Sebastian pulled down on the edges of his waistcoat and then sat. His stomach, quiet before, reacted to the aromas from Cook's fragrant carrot teacake.

Looking at one of his pendulum clocks, he noted the time. Two o'clock. He had worked straight through the nuncheon hour of midday. He was hungry.

The word "hungry" brought to mind his godson, who also happened to be his nearest neighbor, except for Mr. Albert McCall to the west of Eversham Hall.

"Tell me, Dobbins, Baron Hungerford has been gone these past two years from his estate, what? He signed up with the Navy and went overseas to assist in that demmed skirmish with the Colonies. Last I heard he was promoted to commander. In charge of his own ship--a sloop of war. Has Hungerford returned from his duty?"

"Indeed he has, Your Grace." Dobbins shook out the linen napkin and draped it over Sebastian's lap. "Just last week his lordship returned to London on a packet boat. At present he is convalescing at Hungerford Park."

"Convalescing? Devil take it! What happened?"

"Commander Walker, or rather Lord Hungerford, was unfortunately wounded in a savage attack two months ago, I believe. The incident occurred in one of those provincial, backwater towns across the ocean, Your Grace."

"By Gad!" To steady his nerves, Sebastian paced the tight area of his bungalow. He liked the lad. As much as he liked anyone, he supposed. Hungerford had to be at least thirty. Or one and thirty. Always had been a plucky youngster. As brave as any fellow Sebastian had ever encountered.

Basil Walker, the Baron Hungerford, had always been an active young buck. Perhaps he was blue-deviled with this convalescing of his. If so, he might be amenable to boarding the *Tempus Fugit*. He might be amenable to seeing how Sebastian's newly created device manipulated time.

Sebastian placed his hand on his butler's shoulder. "How is Lord Hungerford faring? What kind of injury did he suffer?"

Dobbins' droopy cheeks reddened like overripe tomatoes. He dropped his gaze to the floor. "I cannot say for certain, Your Grace, but I have heard his lordship sustained a bullet wound to his... er, buttocks region. An incensed Colonial damsel fired a large caliber gun or musket in his direction."

The devil!

Coughing to hide his amusement, Sebastian then took a sip of tea. "I see. Perhaps Lord Hungerford has tired of vegetating. I shall issue an invitation to him for the morrow. He might enjoy a bit of sea air on my schooner, what? There he can... rest on his laurels, as it were."

Then Sebastian laughed which gave Dobbins permission to smile as well.

After consuming the refreshments, Sebastian gestured for his butler to remove the debris. Once he was alone, excitement bubbled in his veins. He could not wait to start the experiment. Finally, after all these years!

Indeed, he was feeling ten times better than he had in a very long time. How could he wallow in the dreary feeling of loneliness when, in the company of his godson, he was close to blowing the top off of time itself?

Order today at Amazon.com.

# About The Author

Award-winning author Susanne Marie Knight specializes in Romance Writing with a Twist! She is multi-published with books, short stories, and articles in such diverse genres as science fiction, Regency, mystery, paranormal, suspense, time-travel, fantasy, and contemporary romance. Originally from New York, Susanne lives in the Pacific Northwest, by way of Okinawa, Montana, Alabama, and Florida. Along with her husband and the spirit of her feisty Siamese cat, she enjoys the area's beautiful ponderosa pine trees and wide, open spaces--a perfect environment for writing.

For more information about Susanne, please visit: her website at: http://www.susanneknight.com.

# Books By Susanne Marie Knight

Amazon.com: http://www.amazon.com/author/susanneknight

**ANCIENT ROME TIME TRAVEL ROMANCE**

A SESTERCE FOR HER THOUGHTS

**REGENCY ROMANCE**

A CONTINENTAL MARRIAGE

THE CONTRARY CONTESSA

THE MAGIC TOKEN

A NOBLE DILEMMA

PAGING MISS GALLOWAY

RELUCTANT LANDLORD, THE

"A Very Special Christmas Present"--short story

**REGENCY TIME TRAVEL ROMANCE**

A DELICATE CONDITION

HAVE CHRISTMAS CARD... WILL TRAVEL

AN IMPOSSIBLE ALLIANCE

"Lady Elizabeth's Excellent Adventure"--short story

LORD DARVER'S MATCH

THE QUESTING BOX

A CAIXA MÁGICA--Versão em Português

REGENCY SOCIETY REVISITED

SOJOURN THROUGH TIME

TIMELESS DECEPTION

AN UNUSUAL MASQUADE

WISHING FOR A DUKE (New!)

**PARANORMAL ROMANCE**

THE AWAY PLACE--Fantasy

COMPETITORS!

THE COMING

"Family Secrets"--short story

GRAVE FUTURE

A KARMIC CONNECTION

MY FAVORITE GHOST

PAST INDISCRETIONS

"Shades Of Old Glory"--short story

"Special Delivery"--short story

THE TWO OF CUPS IS FOR LOVERS

UNCOVERING CAMELOT--Fantasy

THE WAKEFIELD DISTURBANCE

**CONTEMPORARY ROMANCE**

THE AWAY PLACE--Fantasy

Carla's One-Sided Crush"--short story

"Friday Night"-- short story

"Grand-mère's Sainte Bleu"--short story

"Happy Anniversary"--short story

LOVE AT THE TOP

MY FAVORITE GHOST

OFF THE GRID--Suspense

QUANTUM KISSES

ONE WIFE TOO MANY

SIGNATURE OF A QUEEN--Mystery

"Teacher's Pet"--short story

"True Love And Candy Corn"--short story

THE TWO OF CUPS IS FOR LOVERS

UNCOVERING CAMELOT--Fantasy

"Zeus And The Single Teacher"--short story

## MYSTERY/SUSPENSE ROMANCE

THE BLOODSTAINED BISTRO (Minx Tobin Murder Mystery, Case 1)

BREAKS AN EGG (Sedona West Mystery, Book 2)

COMPETITORS!

THE DUPLICITOUS DIVORCE (Minx Tobin Murder Mystery, Case 3)

THE EMBEZZLED ENVELOPE (Minx Tobin Murder Mystery, Case 6)

FLIRTING CAN BE MURDER

THE ILL-GOTTEN INSURANCE (Minx Tobin Murder Mystery, Case 2)

OFF THE GRID--Suspense

PUSHES UP DAISIES, (Sedona West Mystery, Book 3)

SIGNATURE OF A QUEEN

SLEEPS WITH THE FISHES (Sedona West Mystery, Book 1)

TAINTED TEA FOR TWO

THE VIRTUAL VALENTINE (Minx Tobin Murder Mystery, Case 4

THE YULETIDE YORKSHIRE (Minx Tobin Murder Mystery, Case 5)

## SCIENCE FICTION/SCIENCE FICTION ROMANCE

"Adolescence"--short story

ALIEN HEAT--Dystopian, Post-Apocalyptic

AN ALIEN PARADISE (formerly entitled XANADU FOR ALIENS)

"The Convert"--short story

THE ENTITLED

FOREVVER

"Homesick"-- short story

JANUS IS A TWO-FACED MOON

JANUS IS A TWO-HEADED GOD

"Saturation Point"--short story

"Special of the Week"--short story

STOPPING THE ENEMY--Dystopian, Post-Apocalyptic

## HORROR

"Cup O'Joe"--short story

## REFERENCE

THE CREATIVE WRITING WORKBOOK

Printed in Great Britain
by Amazon

27335175R00101